$17.00

d.
.00

MW00987800

WE LOOK LIKE
MEN OF WAR

WE LOOK LIKE
MEN OF WAR

★   ★   ★

William R. Forstchen

A Tom Doherty Associates Book
New York

This is a work of fiction. All the characters and events portrayed in this novel are either fictitious or are used fictitiously.

WE LOOK LIKE MEN OF WAR

Copyright © 2001 by William R. Forstchen

All rights reserved, including the right to reproduce this book, or portions thereof, in any form.

This book is printed on acid-free paper.

Design by Jane Adele Regina

A Forge Book
Published by Tom Doherty Associates, LLC
175 Fifth Avenue
New York, NY 10010

www.tor.com

Forge® is a registered trademark of Tom Doherty Associates, LLC.

Library of Congress Cataloging-in-Publication Data

Forstchen, William R.
We look like men of war / William R. Forstchen.
p.   cm.
ISBN 0-765-30114-8
1. United States—History—Civil War, 1861–1865—African Americans—
Fiction.   2. African American soldiers—Fiction.   3. African American boys—
Fiction.   I. Title.
PS3556.O7418 W4   2001
813'.54—dc21   2001040446

First Edition: December 2001

Printed in the United States of America

0 9 8 7 6 5 4 3 2 1

For the Reverend Garland White and the men of the 28th United States Colored Troops; and for Professor Wendy Kasten, Kent State University, who pushed me for so many years to bring this story to life

Acknowledgments

My special thanks must go to the staff at the Indiana State Archives for their generous help while researching this project and the doctoral dissertation that evolved out of it, Elizabeth Pearson of the Montreat College library, and Brian Thomsen, trusted editor and friend.

"The historian's pen cannot fail to locate us somewhere among the good and great, who have fought and bled upon the altar of their country."

—Major Garland White,
chaplain, 28th United States Colored Troops

"In our youths our hearts were touched with fire."

—Oliver Wendell Holmes, Jr.

WE LOOK LIKE
MEN OF WAR

Chapter 1

★ ★ ★

Indianapolis, Indiana
June 1895

I was born a slave, as was my father before me, but I shall die a free man. The words sound wonderful when they roll off your tongue—*a free man*. You almost want to bite into the words and chew on them for a while, to taste their sweetness, and their bitterness. You get the urge to say them real slow, almost afraid that they might just up and disappear on you.

The word *freedom* certainly has an awe-inspiring power to it. I don't think white folks really understand just how powerful it truly is. They were, after all, born to it, they live with it, and they die comfortable in it.

Now for us black folk, we know different. We know just how powerful the word *freedom* really is. For two hundred and forty long years we did not have it. Like Moses' people we were lost in the Egypt of our bondage. And when we broke the chains at last, we paid with our blood for the getting of it.

I should know, because I was there and paid my price in full for what little piece of freedom I now have.

Maybe you saw me marching in the Decoration Day parade last week. As I marched in that parade I found it hard to believe it's the thirtieth anniversary since the Civil War ended. The time has flowed like a river, as I guess it does with all lives. It seems to move sluggish at first, meandering along as if every day will stretch into an eternity. And then, ever so imperceptibly, it moves faster and faster. You're fourteen and you march off to war, somehow believing in your immortality, and with that first thundering volley that illusion is killed forever. But time still seems to go slow. You get a bit older, marry, have children, start a job, and then one day you turn around and there is gray in your beard and a slowness in your step. You look back at what was and shake your head as if it was a dream—only yesterday, you say; but that yesterday was thirty years past.

So I marched in the Decoration Day parade again.

General Howard, who started the college I went to, marched in this one, right down Market Street, a whole flock of other old generals and colonels right along with him. That fellow who wrote *Ben-Hur*, Lew Wallace from over Crawfordsville, he was a general too during the war and he was marching up front as well. They were followed by the boys who fought with them through four long and bitter years of Civil War. Our battle flags were held up to the wind again, powerful names written upon them in fading gold letters, the names of battles like Gettysburg, Antietam, Chickamauga, Shiloh, Petersburg, where I was, and Appomattox.

So there up front were the generals and the white soldiers right behind them. And forgotten, way in the back of the parade came us black soldiers. You see, even though we bled with them and died with them, it seems now they don't quite want us marching with them. But every May 30 we come out anyhow for the parade, the few of us still left, and we march in the parade too, invited or not. Maybe it's cussedness on our part, but I think it's because we want to remind folks that blacks fought in the war too, and died in the war.

I admit we're getting old now; a lot of us boys are getting gray in the beard and a bit bald on top. But when we put the blue Yankee suits on, smelling of mothballs, it all comes back, like it's in the blood somehow. You can almost hear the sergeants cussing at us again, you can almost feel the cool breeze of morning as we stood in line, waiting for the order to charge, the thunder of the cannon booming all around us. We stand a little straighter again, laughing when one of us has a hard time buttoning up his uniform, our backs cracking when we hear the long roll of the drums and snap to attention.

So you might have seen me way in the back of that parade. I was the one with a drum slung over my shoulder, my empty left sleeve pinned up across my breast. An old one-armed drummer, I guess, is kind of a queer sight. But I'm getting ahead of myself and maybe I should tell you it in the way it happened, rather than all backwards the way I'm telling it right now.

My name is Samuel Washburn. At least, that's the name I go by now. You see, it wasn't my birth name and the name they said over me when the preacher dunked me in the river. Why, then I was just plain Sam, though some called me Sambo, or the Washburn family's newest nigger.

Like I said before, I was born a slave. As near as I can reckon now it was in the year 1849 or maybe 1850.

Now you might be wondering: Sam, if you were born a slave, how come you can write a decent hand and folks call you a lawyer? Well, all that in its proper time.

My ma was a house slave, working inside the Washburns' big house. She was able to wear some fine clothes, for a slave, the cast-off's of the Missus. She never was hit either, at least while old Massa Washburn was alive. My pa was a free man, a blacksmith no less, living in Perryville, Kentucky.

He'd been born a slave too on the Washburn farm. But he learned himself a trade and after doing all the blacksmithing work for the Washburns, they'd hire him out to other white folks who needed things done, like shoeing horses, making tools, putting iron rims on wagon wheels and such. In what little time he had left at the end of the day he'd make a couple of extra things. He could turn out a real fine lightning rod or a weather vane that was all so fancy, and Massa Washburn let him sell these things. Half the barns and houses around Perryville must have had one of Pa's lightning rods on them and never one of them burned from lightning (though they sure didn't keep the Yankees from burning them down when the war came).

He worked for near on to twenty years, never spending even two bits on himself come Sundays. He worked and saved and he finally bought himself into freedom for all of fifteen hundred dollars. Massa Washburn even gave him a little piece of land at the edge of town to live on in exchange for his doing some of the chores around the farm. So Pa set himself up as a smithy and was saving money again to buy Ma out of slavery. You see, if it wasn't for Ma, Pa would have gone north over the Ohio River when he bought his freedom. Being a free black man in Kentucky wasn't the best of things, especially with the troubles starting, but he loved Ma and wouldn't leave her behind. Sad thing was that there wasn't just Ma after I came along and so he was going to have to buy me too. I had two sisters, but both of them died of the cholera. It was sad; Ma would cry anytime their names were mentioned, though I don't recall it since I was only three when it happened. At least Pa wouldn't have to buy their freedom as well.

Finding out you're a slave is a strange sort of feeling. I grew up alongside Ben Washburn, he being my age, the only son of Massa and Missus Washburn. All the rest of their children were girls and a lot older than us.

Ma was his mammy and nursed him same as me. We played together out on the front porch on warm summer days. We'd play Indians. My big cousin Jimmie, who was born of Ma's sister who died birthing him, and I would be the Indians and Ben would be George Washington or Daniel Boone. We always lost.

I think I was about five, maybe six or so when one day I got awful mad at Ben and said I wanted to win for a change. He laughed at me and said I couldn't win since I was a stupid nigger slave.

I got mad and punched him hard in the eye. Now, it wasn't anything, just a little boy's punch that could barely hurt a fly, but he started into bawling and ran into the big house. Out came his mama with my ma right behind her. And I saw that my ma was awful scared, her eyes wide, and she was wringing her apron up into knots of worrying. It was a queer sort of feeling. I could see my ma was scared to death of the Missus and it seemed as if everything in the world got terribly quiet, everybody stopping to see what was going to happen.

I thought Missus Washburn would take my arm right off of me when she yanked me off the ground. She picked me up and shook me till it felt like my head was about to burst and I couldn't see all too well.

And Ma just stood there, crying softly, and I saw she was afraid. I started screaming for Ma to make her stop but Ma just stood there frozen, all pale and shaky. Missus Washburn finally threw me back down on the ground, where I landed hard on my head, and then she turned to my ma.

"If your little nigger brat ever lays hands on my boy again I'll sell both of you down south."

Ma tried to open her mouth to say something but no words could come out of her and she just stood there shaking.

Well, this was one big commotion. Everybody saw it. I noticed the other black folks, and there was about twenty of them living on the Washburn farm, were standing very quiet, not saying anything. Massa Washburn came around from the back of the house and asked what all the fuss was about. The Missus just laid into him, shouting that he was too easy on his niggers, that they needed firm treatment. He tried to make her calm down and go back into the house and she started yelling even louder.

He got real mad then, but it wasn't at her who was causing all the fuss but rather at us. He cursed and shouted at Ma to get out of sight and take me along. Ma swept me up off the ground and ran.

I guess I was pretty badly hurt. I had fevers for a while, got real dizzy when I tried to stand up and threw up anything Ma tried to put into me.

Pa came to see me on Sunday visiting day and I saw him standing outside our cabin talking with Massa Washburn, their voices low. Pa seemed vexed, his head bowed as Massa Washburn talked angrily and then went away.

My pa came into our cabin. Ma started into crying and he held her, making hushing sounds. He came over to where I was lying on our cornhusk mattress and sat down by me, putting his hand to my head.

Pa was a big and powerful man and afraid of nothing. He'd go into a stall with the meanest mule, talking soft to it, and next thing you knew he'd have four new shoes on him and the mule just eating sugar out of his hand. His arms were like twin knots of solid hickory wood, his chest as strong as iron barrel hoops. But he could be the gentlest man you'd ever know. I never once heard him rise his voice to Ma, never once saw him put a hand to her, except to touch her gently. He was the same with me and I'm not ashamed to admit that even after forty years I still love him and still get a bit damp in the eyes when I think of him.

He talked with me for a long time that morning and I never forgot it. He told me a lot of things, about being colored or white, slave or free, servant or master. I guess it was troubling for him because I asked the simple questions that little ones ask, which so often cut into the heart of how crazy our world sometimes is.

"Why are we slaves and they're free?"

"What does Jesus say about these things? The preacher keeps saying we're supposed to love each other."

"Does God hate colored folks 'cause we're slaves and the white folks aren't?"

Pa tried to answer the questions, and as I asked them he'd sometimes sigh, chuckle softly, his deep voice rich and smooth.

He'd shake his head and say, "I don't know, son. I don't think even Preacher Wilson knows the answer to that one."

I remember that day all so well, as clearly as if it happened just yesterday. The air was soft with the touch of spring. The grass in the fields was coming up a dark rich blue green. The apple orchards were blooming, their white petals filled with a soft sweet smell of living. It was a Sunday morning when you wanted to be all so glad to be alive. You wanted to run through the fields just laughing, take a sip of icy water from a dark, deep pool of springwater and then lie on your back and watch the clouds float by, hoping you might catch sight of an angel sitting on top of one.

Yet it was a dark, chilly type of day inside of me. I was learning just how the world really was that spring morning. I was learning the meaning of words like *slave* and *free*. I was learning the dark hate that lingered behind the word *nigger* and the sadness inside so many folks, even inside the white folks who thought they ruled us, but down deep were maybe just a bit afraid of us as well.

I think every child, black, white, Indian, or whatever, must have that day in their soul. The day they learn that there is a world beyond their front door, a world not of smiles and laughter and love, but sometimes of darkness, and fear, and cold, evil things that twist through our souls.

It was early in the evening when he left us to go back to his little shop. Before he left he kissed me on the forehead, and pulled a little hard sugar candy out of his pocket and gave it to me.

I remember that day all so well. I remember it for all so many reasons, especially because it was the last time I ever saw my pa alive.

I woke up the following morning and heard Ma crying. Massa Washburn was standing outside the cabin with her and it sounded like he was crying as well. I got up and peeked out the door and saw him standing with Ma, and he even had his arm around her shoulder as she cried. A whole bunch of folks were gathered around them, and there lying on the porch of Massa's house was Pa.

He was dead.

It seemed that when Pa left us he took a back road to town. It was getting dark out and there on the road he was stopped by slave catchers. Now, things were getting all stirred up in Kentucky in those days. More and more slaves were breaking free and running north, trying to get across the Ohio to freedom. And slave owners from down south were paying slave catchers to go after them.

Four of these slave catchers stopped my pa and said he

looked like a runaway down from Nashville way. Pa got his freeman's paper out and said he was not a slave and that they could go to Massa Washburn's place and he'd prove it.

They laughed; one of them got some chains and said, Freeman or not, you're a good-looking nigger and we'll get two thousand dollars for you down in Mississippi. Pa knocked the one man down and started to run . . . and they shot him in the back.

He crawled back to Massa Washburn's and died on the porch there after telling the Massa what happened.

I don't really remember that much; a lot of what I think I remember is stuff my ma and others must have told me later. What I do recollect for sure was seeing my pa lying inside a coffin as they nailed the lid shut and then put him into the ground. It was raining hard, like the whole world was crying because a good man had died. Preacher Wilson prayed over the hole in the ground, saying that Pa was sitting with Jesus and the angels now. But all I could see was a rain-soaked box, the mud splattering as they shoveled the dirt in on top of him.

Ma said I was sick for a long time later and it was awful strange because I went for a couple of years and never said a word. People thought I was struck dumb from grief and getting my head shaken into a concussion. I guess I just didn't have anything to say to the world, that's all.

Massa Washburn was really angry about it all and even had the patrol men from down south arrested. Some white folks, I'm told, laughed about it, but there was a lot of good in Massa. There were a lot of other white folks who were angry too since they thought rather highly of Pa and said he was a good man. Massa Washburn even had them brought to trial. They were fined twenty-five dollars each for killing a freeman and then they were let go and told to get out of the county. Strange thing was that if Pa had still been Massa Washburn's slave they'd have been fined Pa's full value of fifteen hundred dollars. Back then a nigger as a slave was worth more than one who was free.

I guess I could say that's when my being a child ended. Though I couldn't speak for the longest time, Massa Washburn had me go to work in the barn, helping to tend the horses that he raised. I must have talked to them about my troubles in a quiet sort of way because I've always liked horses ever since, more than people sometimes.

I worked in that barn for close on to eight years. I finally started into talking again; it happened the night the barn caught on fire and I had to get help. I ran to Massa Washburn's big house and started screaming there was a fire. They saved the barn and the animals and he said I was a good boy. I guess Massa Washburn was a bit partial to me because of the way my pa died and then me saving his barn and horses like that.

Even now, after all these years, I still think kindly of him, but of his son, Ben, I think he was the devil himself and that's why I finally left, because of him . . . and because the war finally came.

Chapter 2

★　　★　　★

The troubles before the coming of the war were like a summer storm building up on the other side of the mountain. The air gets mighty still and hushed and you get a feeling in your bones that something's about to break. When a storm like that is coming, animals know it for certain: a horse will get really fidgety and nervous, birds will settle into the trees and rabbits head for their holes.

It was the same thing, in a way, with a war coming on. You could feel the tension just building. On occasion Massa Washburn would take me into town when he was going to fetch something and I'd ride in the back of the wagon. I'd hear snatches of talk on the streets. For the first time I heard about far-off places like Kansas, where men who had slaves, and those who didn't, were fighting. Then, in the fall of 1859 there was all this talk about a fellow named John Brown and how he tried to get us slaves to take up guns against the white folks way over in Virginia.

That made a real stir. The patrols were out in force on all the roads and no black, free or slave, would dare to travel alone, elsewise he would get arrested and maybe even beat up. Later I heard how whole towns and counties would suddenly get convinced that there was a rebellion being planned, or that

Yankee abolitionists were coming to make trouble and all the white folks would get out their guns. More than one black man found himself roughed up or even on the end of a rope in those days, out of people's fears that some dark plot of slave revolt was getting planned.

At night we would gather in old Preacher Wilson's cabin and talk in low whispers. Some said they were thinking of running for the Ohio River, going north to freedom land. Others talked to how Harriet Tubman was sneaking into the South and stealing slaves away and taking them to freedom up north. Two folks from the Truddle farm over next to us even did try for a run. They were caught right on the banks of the Ohio when the patrols saw them stealing a boat to cross over with. They were beat horribly, according to the preacher, and sold the next day down to Mississippi. We all heard that if you were sent to Mississippi it was as good as dying since you might get worked in the swamps, draining land filled with fever, alligators and snakes.

Preacher Wilson told us to sit tight and not go looking for trouble, that the Lord would deliver us by and by. We started to hear another name as well, the name of Abraham Lincoln. Everyone knows now that he was born right in Kentucky, not forty miles from where I lived. That alone got a lot of white folks in our parts stirred up, saying he was a traitor to his own kind.

Being alone out there on the farm we only got what we called "half news" of what was going on in the whites' world. I didn't even really know what a president was. I figured he was sort of like a master except more powerful and lived in a big mansion with hundreds of acres of tobacco and fields for horses that stretched as far as the eye could see.

When we's heard that Lincoln was to be the president we also heard all this dark talk that now war was for certain. It gave us a strange sort of hope, but it made me scared as well. I almost believed that I'd wake up one morning and like in the Bible there'd be armies with chariots and horns and such just fighting away in our back pasture. It makes me want to laugh in a sad sort of way when I think how innocent I once was, back when I was a slave boy and knew no better. The preacher kept telling us Bible stories about the first Abraham and how he was the leader of his people and this made the second Abraham seem like a character out of the Bible. Late at night Preacher would tell us how one day Abraham would come on a fiery chariot and with sword in hand set us free.

That winter of 1860 passed into the spring of 1861 and you could almost feel the dark clouds coming to blot out the sun from the heavens. You could hear the white folks talking about something called secession and how Kentucky was caught right in the middle. There were all sorts of meetings in near every town deciding whether they were for this secession or whether they were going to be Union men now that Lincoln was to be the president.

Massa would ride into Perryville for these meetings and he was a big leader for the secess cause. He even got himself a uniform and my ma helped to stitch on the fancy gold buttons that were special-ordered all the way from New Orleans. It was a fine-looking uniform, with gray trousers and blue stripes down the sides. It was all topped off with a dark gray jacket and a black hat with a big white plume in it. We all thought he looked really fine, though he did have trouble walking with his sword on and kept tripping over it, but none of us dared laugh.

And then there came a warm quiet day in April, almost like the one years before when my pa died. It was a Sunday morning and we were doing our chores before the preaching. And then we heard the sound of church bells ringing all the way from town.

Massa Washburn came out of the house, his missus with him, and they looked nervously towards town. He said that it was strange to be ringing the bells so early and all of them together. He had me get a horse saddled up and then he rode into town to see what all the commotion was about.

Some of the folks from the Truddle farm came over, their massa allowing them to come on Sunday to hear Preacher Wilson, and one of them said that the bells meant that the white folks were having a war.

A couple of hours later Preacher Wilson was going into his sermon when we saw Massa Washburn coming back to the house, riding hard, and the Missus ran out to meet him. He said something and she started to cry, but Ben started to jump up and down really excited, whooping and hollering.

Massa called Preacher over and told him to gather us around and we stood in front of the porch of the big house.

"A war has started," he began, and the Missus turned and ran back into the house crying. "The Yankees have started a fight down in South Carolina and the south will fight them. Now, I've been asked to be captain of a company and I'm leaving here today to join the army. I expect you people to behave. Missus Washburn will see after things and my son will too. I expect you people to behave yourselves and I'll get a full report on each and every one of you when I come back."

"How long you gonna be gone for, Massa?" Preacher asked.

Massa chuckled softly.

"Them Yankees ain't worth a pinch of owl dung," Massa said. "It'll be over before the corn's even ready for harvest."

Lord, how I laugh now when I think of them words, but then again, I guess everybody, both North and South, thought it was going to be easy.

"Now, you all go back to your praying, and while you're at it put in a word with Jesus that the Yankees don't come this way."

"The Yankees comin' here?" Preacher asked and I knew it was hard for him to hide the hope in his voice.

"They just might try it. And I tell all of you they're like devils so pray they don't show up."

With that Massa went into the house to get some things and we went back to the circle of log benches which served as our church when the weather was good.

We sat around talking and wondering. I have to tell you now I was rather scared. From the way Massa kept talking I sort of pictured the Yankees to be like the slave chasers that killed my pa. Some folks said they might even have horns like the old devil himself. But others laughed and whispered that the Yankees would make us free. Preacher prayed mighty hard and we even put in a word for Massa that he would come safely home.

That might seem strange to you now, praying for the man that owned you, but you weren't there to know what it was really like. That farm was the only world any of us ever knew. Most of us had been born, lived, and would die there. The older folks had been there even back in the days when Massa's pa ran the place. The Washburns were better than most when it came to owning us. They had a rule that they would never split up a family no matter what. They let my pa buy his freedom, which was something not many masters would do.

We knew nothing else. Though I'm ashamed to admit it now I couldn't read a word, couldn't even figure numbers much past ten, and had never traveled further than to Perryville in my entire life. The world I knew was simply a place where Massa was all the power in the world. With him leaving for this war it seemed as if everything was getting turned around backwards.

As owners go they weren't all that bad and only if sorely provoked did they ever hit one of us. At least Massa didn't, though I couldn't say the same for the Missus and for Ben. If I was praying hard for Massa to come back it was because I was afraid of the other two more than anything.

I think when you cut into the heart of what being a slave was, that was it. It was being afraid of someone else who could do anything they wanted to you. I've heard many a terrible story about what masters did to their slaves, some which aren't even fit to be put down on paper or spoken of, like this story. If you've never been a slave you'll never really know what I'm saying. You'll never know what it's like to look at another person and know they can do anything to you, at any time, and you'll just have to take it and no one can help you. I saw that in my ma's eyes on the day the Missus beat me. I saw that terrible fear, my ma afraid that I might even get killed and she couldn't raise a finger to stop it. That's the heart and soul of being a slave, to know you don't even own your own body and maybe even your own soul as well. That another person controls you except when you sleep and run free in your dreams.

As for freedom? It was a strange sort of dream, almost sort of like how I pictured Pa must now be living in heaven. I knew the Yankees had freedom up north, that black folks could even go to school, get book learning and keep what they earned for themselves. I wanted it more than anything in the world, especially the book-learning part. I thought it'd be the finest thing in the world to be able to read out of the Bible myself, and know all that was happening in the world just on the other side of the hills. I wanted that in the worst possible way, but the thought of trying to run for it, to make it to the Ohio, left my blood cold. All I could think about was my pa, a freeman no less, getting shot down in the road and crawling away to die.

A couple of the folks whispered that they were thinking of running north now that there was a war on. I looked over at Ma when such talk started. She shook her head no and whispered to me that she had lost my pa, and no way was she going to risk losing me.

Later that afternoon Massa Washburn came out of the house. He was wearing his fine and fancy uniform, with gold braid on his shoulders and a double row of gold buttons down the front. He had me get his favorite horse, Caesar, all saddled up. I held it for him and he smiled at me and told me to be good. George, the preacher's oldest son, was going with him to be his servant, and I was filled with envy because George was going to see what a war was all about.

We all shouted good-bye and Massa rode up to the house. He leaned over from his saddle, took hold of the Missus and kissed her and we all cheered. And then he rode down the road, George following behind him on a mule.

The war lasted a bit longer than old Massa figured on.

I never saw him again. He was killed at Shiloh and George died of the camp fevers not long after.

They say Massa got a really fine grave; we don't know where they buried George.

In the first year the war didn't trouble us all too much, though for the white folks it was a whole lot of trouble. You see, Kentucky was all divided up over this war. Some folks were for the North, others for the South, and sometimes it was neighbors against neighbors. People who'd been friends all their lives now found themselves carrying guns against each other. Right around where we were the feelings for the South were pretty strong. A lot of the men went off to join the secess army, and others stayed home and formed up a home guard. This was a dark time for the colored folks. We didn't dare leave our homes, and no white master would send a slave out to do a chore or run an errand, afraid that he might run off or get bushwhacked. So we stayed close to home and the world seemed to roll on quietly.

We heard that there was even some fighting in Kentucky,

but we saw nothing of it in that first year, though we heard that a whole group of Yankees marched down the road going from Perryville to Bowling Green, heading south, but we never saw them.

If the war affected me at all it was that the Missus and Ben now were in charge. I was always afraid of the Missus after that beating and stayed far away from the big house. With his pa gone, something seemed to come over Ben. He took to riding out into the fields and though he wasn't any older than me, and I was but twelve then, he took to giving out orders to us and expecting them to be obeyed. The older men did as he told them, though they'd smile a bit and say that the boy was putting on airs, but they'd still lower their heads and call him Massa just to humor him. But there was a dark streak in him, somehow; I think he got it from his ma.

My own ma said that after the Massa left the Missus took to sleeping with a pistol by the side of her bed, saying that if the Yankees didn't get her the niggers would. Ma kept trying to tell her she had nothing to fear from us, but she didn't believe it. I think it rubbed into Ben's hide. He started getting nasty and mean, saying we were lazy, that we were cheating and stealing food and plotting Yankee tricks.

He took to holding a riding crop when he rode around the farm. At first he just waved it at us when he got vexed over something, but then one day he went and hit my cousin Jim on the back of the shoulders with it. Now, Jim didn't say anything, though it was a strange sight to see him, near full grown and almost as big as my pa, getting switched by this white boy who was no bigger than me. Jim finally turned and walked away, but later he said he was afraid that if Ben ever hit him like that again he'd kill him.

That seemed to set something loose in Ben and nearly every day he'd hit somebody. The preacher finally went to Ma and asked her to talk to the Missus and see if something could be done. Ma was scared but she finally did try to talk with the Missus. The Missus got all fired up and slapped Ma, saying that she was getting uppity in trying to tell her how the young master should behave.

The winter and spring of that year were a hard time for us. First off, we lost most of the farm's horses when a man showed up one day with a piece of paper and told the Missus that the government was buying the horses for the army whether she liked it or not. I cried when they took away Cassius and Brutus. I'd helped to raise those two since they were colts and they followed me about like they were puppy dogs. It seems funny now, what with all the dying that I came to see in those times, but I still wonder about those horses, hoping that they somehow made it through the war and got to go back to a farm. War is hell on horses and Lord knows I'd seen enough dead ones by the side of the road when I was in the army.

Word came along in April that a terrible battle had been fought down in Tennessee, at a place called Shiloh, and that a lot of men from around our way were caught up in it.

And then came the news that Massa Washburn had been killed.

His widow near died of the grief and you could hear her wailing late at night. We didn't see her for weeks and when she finally did come out of the house, it was a terrible sight. She seemed to have turned old; there were streaks of gray in her hair, made even whiter-looking because of the black widow's dress and veil that covered her face. It was then that Ben turned terribly ugly and seemed to always be on the point of a murdering rage.

My world was suddenly turned on its ear. At least before, though I was afraid of Ben and the Missus, I knew that Massa kept things in check just by the fact that one day he'd be coming back. That was gone and here we were, twenty-one slaves held in terror of a young man who'd gone dark with hate, somehow blaming us for the death of his pa.

We endured it through the summer of that year and it was like the rest of the world was getting caught up in the hatred as well. There were stories of bushwhacking late at night and barns being burned by neighbors who had come to hate each other. Though for myself I didn't think much about it that summer, because that's the summer I lost my ma.

It was a hot, dusty day, it hadn't rained in weeks, and the sun beat down on us like a hammer on an anvil when we were out in the fields. I saw this fella come riding up to the house and the sight of him set my blood cold. He had a couple of other men with him and they were carrying shotguns, and behind them was a line of thirty slaves or more, each of them chained to the next. They were slave buyers. Now before, whenever they came, Massa would send them away, but times were different now and we all knew that money was short since that's all the Missus and Ben talked about.

We were called in from the fields, made to stand in line, and that fella walked up and down checking on us. He smelled evil and he looked evil with yellowlike skin and yellow teeth with breath that stank of hard liquor. He looked at me, felt my arms, and then said something about my being worth something in a couple of years but what they needed now were strong bucks to work down south.

He stopped in front of Jim and looked him over carefully. Now, if ever sickness was a blessing it was then, for Jim had the pink eye. His eyes were all red and runny and when that buyer saw Jim's eyes he moved on. He pulled out three, though, one of them being Preacher's only remaining son. The Missus and him haggled about the price and it was agreed upon. They were just about to leave when Ma came out onto the porch and one of them saw her.

"How much for that good-lookin' wench on the porch?" one of them asked.

Ma started to back up but the Missus turned, looked at her, and then real quick and mean-like said four hundred dollars in Yankee money. Not twenty minutes later I was hanging on to my ma, crying as if I was about to die. The slave-buying men laughed, tried to push me aside, and I lost my head and started to fight. The next thing I knew I was on the ground and looking straight up into the muzzle of a shotgun, the man swearing that he'd kill me.

Ma got between him and me and shouted for Jimmie to take hold of me. I felt Jim's arms going around me and he pulled me back.

Ma looked me straight in the eyes, held out her hand and touched me on the face.

"Listen to your cousin, Sam, he's gonna be like your pa for you now. Live like the preacher tells you to and I'll meet you and your pa in heaven someday."

They took her away and Jim held me tight, crying almost as hard as I was, since she had raised him as well. She was as gone from my life as my pa was.

Long after the war I went looking for her, but I never did find a trace of where she had gone off to. Now that I'm getting to be an old man I pray every night that when Jesus comes to take me home, Ma and Pa will be standing beside him.

It's kind of hard to remember clearly what all came next in that summer and fall. I took down bad with a case of the typhoid fever and it almost carried me off. The truth is I half wished it would take me off since I really didn't want to live anymore. If it hadn't have been for Jimmie and the preacher I would have died for certain. Jimmie would sit up in the evenings with me, exhausted from working in the fields. He'd nurse me almost as gentle as my ma, wiping the sweat from me, feeding me a broth that the preacher made and telling me stories about how one day we were going to be free, and that we'd find Ma and be a family again.

I started feeling fit again, though I was still as weak as a kitten, and got the shakes if I tried to work too hard. But Massa Ben told me that I had to go into the fields to bring the harvest in with the others and I went out to work. It was getting into the fall of 1862 and one of the worst droughts ever had dried up all the crops and the heat was something terrible. Now, Ben couldn't be everywhere at once, nor could the Missus. So Jimmie would watch out and when they weren't around he'd have me lie in the shade and rest. That was what finally put Jimmie and me on the freedom road and into the war.

We were out bringing in the corn and I got dizzy and had to lie down. Jim thought that Massa Ben was back at the big house and told me it was safe. So I went over to the edge of the field and lay down. We had a signal worked out that when Jim started to whistle it meant that Ben or the Missus was coming. I guess I fell asleep and didn't hear him.

I woke up to someone kicking me hard in the ribs. I let out a yell and rolled over and tried to get away, but I guess I rolled the wrong way and banged straight into Ben and knocked him over.

That's what really did it.

I started to get up and he was down on the ground screaming that I was a dead nigger because I hit him. I was scared to death; I didn't know what was going on. One moment I'd been asleep and the next Ben was screaming that he was going to kill me.

I was so scared I actually went over to him and offered my hand to help him back up, saying I was sorry. He knocked my hand away and told me not to move. He didn't have to tell me not to move, I was frozen to the spot with fear. He went over to his horse, grabbed hold of a riding crop with one hand and pulled a pistol out of his holster with the other and turned back to me. I thought at that moment I was dead for certain.

He walked up to me and looked at me with murder in his eyes. He started talking crazy, saying that his pa had liked me more than him and then said some horrible things about my ma and his pa, and that's why she was sold away first chance after Massa Washburn was killed. Now, I knew about such things back then, you heard stories enough about it, but I can tell you that Massa Washburn wasn't that type of man. I think that it was the Missus who was crazy with brain sickness and started thinking these evil things and it got into Ben's soul and made him crazy as well.

I didn't know what to say. He was talking disrespectfully not only about his dead pa, but about my ma as well. It started to get me boiling mad. White man or not, master or not, I was thinking that this was going too far, speaking such things. I know that in the white man's world to say such a thing about another man's mother—true or not, and I knew it wasn't true—was cause enough for a fight.

I felt all cold inside and somehow distant from myself, as if I was watching Ben and me from far away. I found myself thinking that this is what slavery did to all of us, white folks and colored, making us hate and fear each other, thinking the worst from both sides, and that they were trapped in it as bad as us and they didn't even know it.

"You're a damned liar," I snapped, shocked at my own rage, forgetting even that he had a pistol in his hand.

"You're a dead nigger," he screamed and he brought the pistol up, cocked it and pointed it straight at me.

If you've ever been near the point of death, and I'm not trying to sound like a hero or anything when I tell you I've been there more than once, a strange sort of thing happens to you. Time seems to slow all down and it feels like a second is dragged into an hour. I thought so many things in that second— that I would soon see my pa again, that I wished I could see Ma once more and, even though it seemed kind of sadly funny, that she'd be mighty surprised when Jesus came for her and there I was waiting as well. It seemed like Ben was at the end of a long, dark tunnel, that I could just see him and nothing else. I felt kind of sick with the thought that most likely the last thing I'd ever see in this world was his hate-filled eyes, his face all twisted up with madness.

And then I saw a hand grabbing hold of his arm, pushing the pistol up. I hadn't even realized that Jimmie had snuck up right behind Ben.

The gun cracked off with a thunder roar and I felt a bullet snick past me. Through the gun smoke I heard grunting as the two of them wrestled. Ben started to scream and then I saw Jim punch Ben really hard in the face. Ben crumpled up like a broken doll. He hit the ground and lay very still.

The smoke cleared and there was Jim breathing hard, standing over Ben. I could see that Jim was scared and after the thunder of that gun going off the world seemed terribly still, as if it had taken to holding its breath.

I looked around and saw folks coming from the field, running, and then slowing to a stop, scared, looking at Ben and being really quiet.

I saw a trickle of blood coming from Ben's head and his face was starting to look really pale.

I went over to him, knelt down and touched the blood. He'd hit his head on a rock. My hands started to shake and I put my hand on his chest and couldn't feel anything.

"Jesus, I think you've killed him," I whispered.

"If I hadn't he'd of killed you," Jim replied, still breathing hard, "and I hope I did kill him."

The preacher came up really quietly, knelt down by Ben and put his hand on his chest.

"I can't feel nothin'," the preacher whispered.

He looked over at me and then at Jim.

"He was filled with the devil, he was; I hates to say it, but the world's better off without him."

He picked up the gun, which was lying on the ground, and handed it to Jim.

"You better run for freedom, boy, 'cause there ain't a white jury in this whole state that will say this was an accident."

Jim nodded, unable to speak.

"And you better go too, Sam," Preacher said quietly.

A bit startled, I looked around. I'd dreamed of freedom for years and then all of a sudden it was straight ahead of me and I started to shake a bit.

"You feeling all right, boy?" Jim asked quietly, coming up and putting his arm around me.

I felt really weak all of a sudden; I guess some of it was the typhoid and some of it was being afraid.

"Now listen careful," Preacher said. "Take Ben's horse, pick up the wood trail north of the farm and follow it out past the Truddle place. Beyond that is the Johnston farm; go wide around it. After that I think you should let the horse go; ain't nothing gonna draw quicker attention than two colored boys riding a horse. At least if they try and set a dog after you, you'll be miles away and no trail to pick up. After that stay in the woods during the day and only move at night. There's Yankees north of Perryville but it can't be a sure thing. You boys have killed a white man and they might send you back. You ain't gonna be safe till you've reached the Ohio and get across it. Even then keep a movin' north, get into Indiana land. Now, do you know what a Quaker is?"

We'd heard about them; they were the white folks who didn't believe in slavery and a lot of them helped runaways.

"There's a whole lot of them in Indiana land. Try and find some. Their churches ain't got no fancy bell towers like the other white folks' churches. I heard you can trust them."

Jim looked down at the body on the ground.

"Come with us, Preacher. There's gonna be hell to pay over this."

The preacher laughed and shook his head.

"These old bones can't do it now," he said with a sad voice. "I's thought about it for forty years. Jesus knows I should of done it when my boys and my missus was still young; maybe they'd all still be alive and with me." His voice started to break.

"No, no, you boys go now, and let me bless you first."

We knelt down and he put his hands on our heads.

"Jesus, guide these boys to freedom land. They's good boys and this here killin' was an accident that weren't their fault at all. So look out for them, Jesus, and see them safe out of the land of slavery and across the Jordan River of freedom."

We got to our feet. Preacher smiled, reached deep down into his pocket and pulled out a small purse. He handed it to us.

"There's three whole dollars in there, boys."

Jim tried to hand it back but he wouldn't hear of it.

I looked back to the house and saw that the Missus was standing out on the porch looking our way.

"Get movin' now," Preacher snapped.

Jim went over to the horse and got into the saddle. He reached down and pulled me up behind him. He dug his heels in and the horse reared up a bit and then took off.

I looked back over my shoulder and saw the preacher kneeling down over Ben. I closed my eyes and hung on, scared yet excited. But I still started to cry a bit. I was leaving behind the place where my pa was buried, and where my ma had raised me. Though I was a slave, it was still home. But there was another thought as well, that I was on my way to freedom and never again would I ever be forced to say the word *Massa*.

Chapter 3

★   ★   ★

I think I could spend a week of talking and not tell you all of what happened when Jim and I ran north. But that's not the story I'm interested in telling you right now, so I'll make this part of it short and sweet like the old widow's dance.

We did like the preacher said we should and rode till the end of the day, staying off the main road, weaving through the woods, and then let the horse go. We slept in the woods for half the night. Jim built a tiny fire and we roasted some ears of corn and slept under a big old sycamore tree. Now, that tree kind of bothered me; I still see it in my nightmares. I kept dreaming that Jim and I were hanging from it and Ben was standing underneath it, looking up at us two as we swung, laughing, his dead eyes staring at us.

The moon came up the color of blood and Jim said it was time we moved on. We set out, getting down by the edge of the road and following it. I still felt awfully weak and he had to help me a lot.

Now I guess the good Lord wanted us to escape because he threw something right in our way that made the getting away easy. You see, there was a battle brewing up, which the history books later called the Battle of Perryville, and it was fought just south of where our farm was. Now, years later, after

I learned to read, I studied up on it and can sit down with a map and trace things out and tell you who was where, and why they were fighting at that particular place, but at the time it was a mystery to me.

Just about dawn we came over a low rise and I felt my blood freeze up when I heard the sound of a gun being cocked.

We'd stumbled straight into some Yankee cavalry.

This Yankee was sitting on his horse smack in the middle of the road and he had a gun aimed straight at us. I think he was nearly as scared as we were.

He started to laugh softly and then lowered his gun.

"You boys sure scared me half to death; you're lucky I didn't put a hole through you."

"We's glad you didn't," Jim said quietly, and the Yankee grinned.

"Running away, is that it?"

Jim was quiet.

"I guess you're more contraband. Well, if you boys are runaway contraband you better go hoofing north, 'cause the whole Rebel army's coming straight this way."

We didn't say another word and kept on going.

Pretty soon there were Yankees all over the place and they barely paid attention to us. A couple cursed at us a bit to get out of the way, and one got a bit nasty when he saw the pistol tucked in Jim's belt, saying a nigger shouldn't be allowed to carry a gun, but he didn't do anything.

Some of them were even kind to us, gave us food, and one offered to give us a wagon ride, which I was mighty grateful for since I was more being carried by Jim than walking at that point.

We slept that night near where a regiment of infantry was camped. The wagon driver made us get off, saying he was turning around to haul up some supplies. A soldier had seen us; later on I came to know that he was an officer. He came over to us and asked us where we were from. I guess he could tell we were scared and he said it was all right, that as far as he was concerned we were free men. He said that President Lincoln was fixing to issue something called an Emancipation Proclamation and that pretty soon all slaves would be free. I found out later it didn't apply to us slaves in the border states, but at the time I didn't know.

It was the strangest of feelings, a white man telling me I was free. Jim finally said we were from Perryville. The officer asked us if we'd seen any Rebels and we told him we hadn't, which was all the truth.

He said we were lucky, that there was a battle shaping up round there and the place would soon be crawling with Rebs. He could see I was feeling poorly and next thing I knew he told a couple of his men to find us some blankets and food. They didn't seem too happy about it, but it was the strangest thing to see a couple of white soldiers looking to find things for us, and we didn't know what to say.

The food was simple army food: hardtack, salted pork, some roasting ears taken from a farm, and coffee. I think it was one of the best-tasting meals of my life and I felt as if strength was coming back into me with every bite.

I sat there watching them as they talked and sang, and then they got quiet and went to sleep. I felt my eyes starting to sting. I didn't know who these men were. But tomorrow they were going to fight. I know long after that some of them fought because they hated slavery and others fought to save the Union, and some didn't like blacks any more than the slave owners did. But they were going to fight and because of them, I was a free man. I thought of my pa, a man who had never hurt anyone and who worked all his life to buy himself free. That struck me as so powerfully sad. My pa had been reduced to buying himself the same way you'd buy a shirt or shoes, a horse or a dog. And he died while trying to buy my ma and me into freedom.

And now the men and boys sleeping around me were going south and some of them were going to die before another day was over. I felt angry and ashamed. I thought they were doing something for me that I should be doing for myself.

I went to sleep thinking on that.

I woke up to the sound of soldiers coughing and opened my eyes. The blanket was warm and wrapped around me, Jimmie's blanket on top of me as well, and he was sitting there tending a small fire. He smiled and offered me a cup of coffee and some more salt pork. The coffee tasted wonderful, not the roasted chicory we slaves drank, but the real thing. Mixed in was some genuine sugar and, strangest thing of all, some milk from out of a can, which I just thought was the most wondrous and funniest thing I'd ever seen. I could just picture someone milking a cow with that little can underneath her.

"They's moving up to fight the secess," Jim said quietly. "That captain fella said we better keep movin' north. Said that there's gonna be a hell of a fit and if they should lose it'd go bad on us if we got caught with them. He said the road north is safe, just stick close by with the wagons."

We heard shouts and the Yankee soldiers all started to get into lines to march, loading their gear up on their backs. The captain came over to us and smiled. He gave each of us a canvas haversack loaded with food, told us to keep our blankets and said that some of the boys with the regiment had thrown in a couple of dollars as well to see us along.

I suddenly blurted out that I wanted to go with 'em, to go back and fight. He looked at me wide-eyed, laughed, and some of the men who were listening started to laugh as well.

"Maybe when we're all dead, then you darkies can fight," one of them said.

"Yeah, and they'll all run away," another man said and again they laughed.

That hurt.

The captain smiled at me.

"Maybe your time will come, boy," he said softly, "but for right now get yourself north to freedom."

"I'll come back someday a soldier," I said and again they laughed.

They started out onto the road and disappeared into the mist of morning. I never did know where they came from and what regiment they were, since I couldn't read the names on the flags back then. The following day they fought the Battle of Perryville. From there they most likely went on to Chickamauga, Missionary Ridge, Atlanta, and down with Sherman to the sea. I hope the captain and most of them made it back, but in my heart I know that only a few of them got out of it alive.

Jim and I headed on north and we fell in with a supply train and followed along. Those mule drivers were mean cusses, and they swore at us, the mules and everything else. They were the foulest-mouthed men I'd ever heard and I bet the preacher would have trembled at some of their words. They weren't like the captain and the soldiers we first met, and kept telling us to clear out. But we hung close anyhow and there was a steady trickle of runaways like us following them as well. There were old folks and young ones, men and women, house servants and tough old field hands, all of us following the North Star to freedom. We sang a lot, songs like "Follow the Drinkin' Gourd" and "Roll, Jordan, Roll."

It was over a hundred miles to the Ohio River and after five days on the road we reached Louisville. It made me think of the stories Preacher told us about the Israeli children and how Moses took them to the River Jordan.

Now, just outside Louisville we met some men and women who we found out later were with the Sanitation Commission. They gave us food and told us not to go into the city unless we stayed close to the soldiers because there were reports that slave catchers were still on the prowl.

Jim said quietly that we'd die before allowing that. We had tasted of freedom and it was as sweet as fresh springwater and never again were we going to drink of slavery.

We followed a line of supply wagons down into Louisville, and in all my life I'd never seen anything like it. Why, there were buildings there that were stacked four, even five floors high, one on top of the other so that you had to crink your neck to look up at them. Everywhere there were people pushing and shoving, laughing, talking, cursing, singing, carrying things, pushing wheelbarrows and moving like they had the most important business in the world. The streets were clogged with wagons, carriages, horses, mules, pigs, sheep, goats and cows. And down by the river it was a sight to behold. Riverboats, looking like they were made out of white cake frosting, lined the bank two and three deep, and when their whistles started to shriek you had to clap your hands over your ears, they were so loud.

We moved along the river, both of us keeping our eyes peeled wide open, just afraid that at any second someone would reach out and snatch us, saying we'd killed a white man and they'd hang us on the spot. But it just didn't happen. There was too much else going on. Everywhere we heard people talking about the big fight down in Perryville, how the secess were retreating and how the war would soon be over. Next to a place where they printed newspapers there was a big blackboard hung on the side of the building and someone would climb up and write out the latest news with chalk.

Boys came out of the building shouting that they had the latest news. I finally convinced Jim to give me three cents and

I bought one of the papers. The boy laughed at me and said I couldn't read, but he sold it to me anyhow and I just looked at it. I knew there were all sorts of things in those lines of mysterious-looking print, ready to tell me about the fighting, and maybe there were lines of writing that would say look out for two runaways who'd killed their master. I actually felt an ache because I couldn't read those words and other folks could. I folded up that paper and put it in the haversack the army captain had given us.

We walked along the river, trying to figure out some way of getting over it, when we saw where a train car was pulled up. They were taking down wounded and sick soldiers from the car and laying them on a wharf.

Some of them were asking for water and we stopped to look at them. I went up to one of the soldiers and he asked me if I could get him some water. I looked around, saw a rain barrel and went over to it, filled up my tin cup and brought it back to him. Next thing I knew all of them were asking for water. They looked terribly sick and I was scared because some of them didn't have an arm or a leg and there was a sweet kind of smell around them that made your stomach start to quiver. But I kept going back to the barrel, bringing them water, and Jim helped me. We no sooner got done with the last when the first one asked for more and we started in again. While we were doing this a ferryboat came up to the dock and they started loading the soldiers on. The first one that asked for water looked up at me.

"Are you boys contraband?" he asked.

I knew now that meant we were runaways and nodded my head.

"Carry me on board that boat and I'll see you get across."

We lifted up his stretcher real careful-like, carried him up on to the boat, laid him down and then just stood there.

A short, nasty-looking little man came up to us.

"You niggers get off my boat," he snapped.

"They're good boys, they're with us," the soldier said, and the others started into agreeing with him and cursing at the boatman.

"Well, it's two bits apiece for them."

The wounded soldier started to reach into his pocket but Jim reached down into his haversack, pulled out a greenback and handed it to the man.

"A nigger with money; well, I'll be damned," said the man and started to turn away.

"Give them their change, don't go cheating them," several of the soldiers shouted.

The man handed us our change back and walked away, cursing at the soldiers and us.

The boat was soon loaded up with soldiers, and with the whistle blowing it started back across the river. I'd never been on a boat before and as we got out into the middle of the river I got kind of nervous. The river was big, at least a mile wide, and the boat kept moving up and down and back and forth, its steam engine huffing and puffing away.

I looked back towards Kentucky and half expected to see the slave hunters standing on the riverbank shaking their fists. I guess that's almost kind of funny now. Here there was a war on, we were inside the Yankee lines and everything was all astir over the battle that had just been fought. But I kept thinking that nearly every person in Kentucky would be personally on the hunt for Jim and me. I guess it goes to show that the biggest problems in the world are usually your own, even when the world is going to hell in a sea of blood from all the fighting and killing.

I looked down at those soldiers, some without arms and legs, and some I could tell were getting set to die. The most important thing for them wasn't two runaway slaves, it was that they were crippled for life, or that they knew they'd never make it home before they died. And it filled me with a terrible sadness. Whether they'd wanted it that way or not, it was more than likely because of them that Jim and I were able to get so clean away. Now, they most likely wouldn't have given a good damn at that moment since they had other things to think about, but it was true anyhow and it filled me with a strange wonder at how the world was changing. I wanted to go and thank each of them for helping to make me free, but I figured they didn't want to be troubled just then.

I felt a little shudder go through the boat and found that I was looking backwards so hard that I forgot to see what was coming forward. We'd docked in Indiana. We were in freedom land.

There was a train waiting there for the wounded, with nurses to look out for them and soldiers to help them get on board the train. Some of them started to cry and said they thought they'd never see the North again.

We got off the boat and watched the soldiers getting loaded on the train. It finally pulled out and away from the dock, heading north, and suddenly we were alone.

We looked at each other. We were in Indiana, we were in the North and we were free. But it was strange now. It was sort of like having a dream and then one day waking up inside the dream, except the world still looks basically the same. There were no different colors to the sky, no angels appearing in chariots to point the way, no streets paved with gold, and the first black man we saw was dressed almost as raggy as we were.

He was sitting on the edge of the dock and we went up to him, cautious-like, and he smiled.

"You boys contraband?

Jim nodded.

The old man's smile widened.

"I could tell, you got that wondering look in your eyes. Now that you're here in freedom land you don't know what to do next."

"I guess that's about the shape of it," I said softly.

He reached over, pulled up a trotline, and hanging on it were half a dozen fat catfish.

"I got some extra for dinner; why don't you come on home with me and maybe we can find a way for you to go."

He took us to his home; it wasn't much more than a shack, but he was proud of it and inside were three young ones and his wife. She said something about bringing more mouths home to feed. Jim said we could move on, but she laughed and told us to sit down.

She set a meal in front of us that made my mouth to water. With the fried catfish we had more roastin' ears, which we pulled out of our haversacks, and even some fresh apple cider and boiled greens, and I ate till I thought I'd burst.

He told us he worked at the docks and fished a bit on the side. He told us that as far as we were concerned it might be safer if we moved a bit further north and followed the railroad tracks up towards Indianapolis. There'd already been a couple of Rebel raids across the river and might be more. The Rebs didn't take kindly to runaways, he said, especially young fellows like us that might be good for some work.

Now, that was a bit of a disappointment to me. I thought that once you got into the North that you were safe forever, and when I said that the old man laughed.

"We ain't never gonna be safe, at least as long as I expect to be alive," he said sadly.

It got me kind of angry to hear that and I didn't like the idea that I'd always have to be afraid.

Then I saw something that really surprised me. The old man lit a lamp, took a book down from a table and put on a pair of silver-rimmed spectacles.

"You can read?"

"Certainly can," he said proudly, and Jim and I looked at him in wonder since he was the first black man we'd ever seen who could read a book.

I reached into my haversack, pulled out the paper and begged him to read from it and tell us all the news of what was going on.

He read to us about the big battle at Perryville and then pointed to a long list of names of men that got killed and I wondered again about the soldiers who helped us. Then he read about the Emancipation Proclamation and how the man who wrote the newspaper didn't like it at all. I asked him about that and he told us how President Lincoln said that all slaves inside the Rebel country would be free as of the first day of the new year but that slaves in Kentucky would still be slaves.

Now that didn't strike me as fair at all and the old man told us a lot about the politics of it and he left me all confused. It seemed that President Lincoln didn't want the white folks in Kentucky, Missouri and Maryland to get all upset so slaves were still going to be slaves there, while slaves everywhere else were free.

He turned the pages and read bits of the news to us and then stopped for a second, looked over at us and smiled.

"You boys did somethin' to your master and that's why you ran away?"

We both froze and looked at each other.

The old man put the paper down on the table and pointed to a small box of print.

"It says right there that two slave boys down near Perryville, one named Sam who's thirteen and still weak from the typhoid, and Jim, seventeen with a scar over his right eye, beat up their master Ben Washburn. They left him for dead, stole his horse, a pistol, and ran away. Washburn is recovering but was close to dying. They're offering fifty dollars' reward for the horse and one hundred dollars for either of you alive and fifty dollars for you dead, no less."

"I thought we killed the dog," Jim blurted out.

We were all silent for a long minute and then the old man started to laugh so hard that he had to take his glasses off to wipe the tears from his eyes.

"Well, I got me a hundred dollars sitting right in this room," the old man said and that got me nervous for a second but I saw that he was still laughing.

"Here we got a war on and they still want you. You boys are lucky someone didn't notice you in all the confusion. That's one mean master who wants you back dead."

Jim told him the whole story and as I listened I got mad again. The things he'd said about my ma I could never forgive and the fact that they'd sold her away was even worse. Part of me was relieved that Jim didn't have the crime of murder resting heavy on his soul, but at the same time I half wished we had killed him anyhow.

"Boys, this settles it. Get yourselves further north. Chances are it'll all be forgotten in a week, but there's a lot of folks, South and North, who don't take kindly to black folks trying to kill white folks. A hundred dollars for two dead colored boys is a lot of money."

"But there's a war on and I guess some of that war is over us," I said. "I'd think that they'd want us to fight in it as well, and I'd be proud to go."

Jim nodded in agreement.

"There's been talk of that, of forming up colored regiments to go fight. Maybe with this here Emancipation Proclamation it might change things, but for right now it's not gonna happen. Now get some sleep and we'll set you on the road come mornin'."

They gave us a corner of their cabin and I fell right asleep. Maybe that was foolish, maybe I should have been worried that the old man might see the hundred dollars more than two folks like himself. But I was tired almost beyond caring.

It was well past dawn after I woke up, the longest I'd ever slept, and I felt better, my strength coming back on again. There was the smell of cornbread cooking and they set a breakfast in front of us and packed our haversacks with enough food to last us till the morrow.

The old man read a bit of the Bible to us and then walked us down to the railroad tracks. We shook hands with him and he gave me my newspaper back. I folded it up real neatly and put it in my bag. It felt kind of powerful having that paper on me since I was locked up in its print.

We started down the tracks and a train came down from the north, its boxcars loaded up with soldiers. We waved as they went past and some of them smiled and waved back. We continued on up the track and not an hour later that same train came back from the river. It came by really slow, the boxcars empty, and Jim shouted for me to run. We ran really fast and he jumped up into an open boxcar and pulled me up after him.

It was the first time in my life I'd ever ridden on a train and it left me breathless. In an hour it'd gone at least twenty whole miles. It was a beautiful fall day; the trees were breaking out into their glory, showing leaves of red and orange and gold. The sky was a deep, deep blue, the air with a faint nip of a chill to it. The sun was warm and we leaned against the side of the open doors, eating cornbread the old man had given us and washing it down with cool water from a canteen. We went through small towns and some folks pointed at us and we waved. Some waved back and others looked kind of angry but the train kept on going and we laughed. A couple of times the train pulled onto a siding to stop so that another train could pass. When this happened we hid in the back of the boxcar until the train started rolling again.

I was free and I was filled with the wonder of it all. Jim and I found ourselves laughing over nothing, singing and joking about how Ben Washburn must be boiling away with anger that we'd gotten clean away.

We kept rolling north, passing small farms that were laid out as neat as could be, the farmers out in the fields bringing in the last of the harvest. The land was flatter than Kentucky, but pleasing to the eye, mixed with long stretches of woods and then open, square fields.

The train was moving right along, going even faster than before, and Jim said we were most likely going all the way to that Indianapolis town that the old man had told us about. So we settled back and watched the land roll by, and with every mile that passed I felt just a little bit safer.

We passed a stretch of houses and some large buildings and we figured we had to be getting into the city. I wasn't sure if I liked this, since we might get caught on the train and I didn't know what the owners of it would think about the two of us sneaking a ride.

A banging shudder went through the train and we heard a whistle blowing. Jim said we better jump off but we couldn't since there was a deep gully on both sides of the track and we would have broken our legs for sure if we'd tried. There were all sorts of houses and streets filled with traffic and the highest church steeples I'd ever seen, but there was nowhere we could jump off.

The train kept slowing down and Jim told me to get ready to jump. I leaned out, afraid to move as we rattled over a wooden bridge. As we reached the other side of the river there were big piles of fresh-cut lumber, stacked up almost clear to the track.

The train groaned to a stop, bell ringing, and we quickly jumped down.

"Hey, you two!"

Scared to death, I looked over my shoulder and saw this heavy-looking man with a long dark beard standing there, hands on his hips.

We started to back up.

"You two. Don't run, I ain't gonna bite."

He started towards us but we kept backing up; he'd take a step and we'd take a step away.

"You want some work?"

I looked up at Jim, ready to follow him if he ran.

"I'm not gonna hurt you. I need some workers; you two look healthy enough."

"What kind of work?" Jim asked quietly.

"Hell, you rode the train, I need someone to load wood on her."

Jim stepped forward nervously and the man smiled.

"Come on, you two, I ain't got all day. I've got trains to load and four of my damn fools didn't show for work today. Now, either you work for me or you don't."

"How much for working, boss?" Jim asked and I was surprised.

"Seventy-five cents a day for you, fifty cents for the little fellow; now take it or leave it, I ain't got all day."

"We'll take it, boss," Jim said and the man smiled.

"Well, don't just stand there, let's get cracking."

After working as a slave you're never afraid of hard work again as long as you live.

Boss's name was Joshua Speed and I think the good Lord was looking over us that day when we ran into him. Later he told us that he always knew he could find good workers by waiting for the first train of the day coming up from Louisville since there was usually at least one or two runaways on it.

He worked us every bit as hard as old Master Washburn did, even harder in a way, but at the end of every day he put six bits in Jim's hand and four bits in mine. We cut and loaded firewood, moved lumber, which the army needed down south, loaded and unloaded boxcars, and on one horrible day we scrubbed out some cars that were bringing wounded back from the war.

He took us to a boardinghouse for colored folks near the railyard. It wasn't anything more than a shack, and when winter came the wind blew right through the cracks in the wall. An old freewoman we called Auntie Hubbard ran the place. She took a liking to us, saying we reminded her of her own boys, who died of the cholera. At the end of the week we still had over two dollars left between us, though really it was Jim's money since room and board for both of us was six and one half dollars a week, but Jim said that half of it was mine anyhow.

The Quaker folks that the preacher had told us about were in Indianapolis, and till the day I die I'll thank them, for it was they who helped me to change from being an illiterate runaway slave into a man who could read and write.

They had a school for colored folks, run by a tiny little spinster lady named Miss Latimer, and after work in the evening and on Sundays I'd go there to learn. I'll never forget the day I first stood up with a McGuffey Reader in my hand and was able to recite a whole page of it and barely make a mistake. It was one of the proudest days of my life.

A whole year passed and I could spend a week telling of all that happened but that, I guess, is another story and I want to get on with this one.

Jim and I worked hard. I went to school and he tried it a bit but said he guessed he wasn't cut out for book learning and finally quit. He kept after me, though, and every night after I

came back from school he'd make me tell him everything I
learned. He even got a piece of slate and some chalk for me
with his own money and had me practice my writing in front of
him before we'd go to sleep. He said that a black man without
book learning was just another field hand, but with book learning I might one day make something of myself.

He was really proud of what I could do after only six
months of school and would tell the other men we worked
with that someday I'd be someone important.

We also met Pastor Garland White, who occasionally vis-
ited our AME church in town. The minister of our church, Pastor Revel, was well known in Indianapolis both with white
folks and black. Besides being a preacher, he was also a doctor,
and not long after the war, his brother became America's first
black senator. Revel and Garland White were good friends, so
whenever Garland was in town, he was always invited to
preach, and his preaching was almost always about the war.

Garland White was a runaway, like me, and belonged to a
famous senator from Georgia, Senator Robert Toombs. Pastor
White fled to Canada before the war and then came back to the
States when the war started. He worked as a recruiter for the
54th and 55th Massachusetts and also for a new black regiment
that was starting up in Rhode Island. Not many people knew
this, but a lot of the men serving with the 54th actually came
from Ohio, and Garland was the one who recruited them. He
was a powerfully built man, with strong hands and deep, pen-
etrating eyes.

It was said how he knew some high and mighty people in
government. He wrote to President Lincoln and to a Mr. Se-
ward, who was the secretary of state, calling on them to orga-
nize black regiments. He was good friends with Frederick
Douglass as well. He sent lots of letters to Governor Morton of
Indiana telling him how the other states were forming black

regiments for the war and it was about time Indiana got into the act.

He got to know me because Miss Latimer came to church to see about getting more students for her school at the same time Garland was visiting. After she finished talking to the congregation, she pointed me out and said how after only six months of schooling, I could already make my way through the second form of the McGuffey Reader and could even handle parts of the Bible.

After the service Reverend White came up to me and shook my hand. He told me how he couldn't read or write a single word only five years ago but studying had opened up a whole new world to him. I told him I wanted to join up for the fight if Indiana ever got around to creating a regiment for black soldiers, and he laughed, saying I had to grow a bit first.

I remember I looked him straight in the eye and said, "How old was David when he fought Goliath? You help start up a regiment here, and Jim and me are joining."

I'll never forget how he put both hands on my shoulders and squeezed them tight, his eyes all serious and not saying a word. Something happened between us at that moment, and I knew that when the time came, I would march along beside him.

During the summer came a lot of news of the war, the worst of it when the big battle was fought at Gettysburg. A regiment from Indianapolis was in that fight and was chewed up really bad. A week or so after the battle the newspaper printed a long, long list of names of the dead and wounded.

It was a terrible time; near on to everybody in town knew somebody who was dead. Worst of all, Mr. Speed's brother was one of them. We took up a collection from all the black workers and I wrote out a note of sympathy, which was printed in the paper. He cried when he read it and thanked us. He used to be a jolly sort of man, but it was a long time before we ever saw him smile again.

A couple of weeks later came news that set all of us into a celebration. A colored regiment had gone to war and fought its first battle. The 54th Massachusetts fought a terrible battle down outside of Charleston. Some folks said we lost the fight and I guess we did, but we won anyhow because we proved to the world that we could fight.

Near to half of the men of that regiment were killed or wounded and their white commander, Colonel Shaw, died leading them. The illustrated newspapers carried pictures of it and even if you couldn't read, you could still stare at the pictures and see black soldiers, in uniform, fighting. One of the soldiers of that regiment received the Medal of Honor for that battle, Sergeant Carey, who carried the flag and was wounded eight times, the first black man in the history of the United States to win that honor.

A couple of months later there was even a poem out and all the papers printed it saying how Shaw, a white man, was honored to be buried with his black comrades in a common grave. I wept when I slowly worked my way through that poem. Though the Quakers don't hold with war, Miss Latimer still let me read it out loud in school, though I still needed help with a lot of the words.

Inside the toolshed at work we even hung up the pictures and the poem and I'd look at it every day. Things started to happen quickly, and suddenly a lot of folks started to say that the 54th had proven something, that black men could fight just as well as white men. And others, who didn't like us, said that if a white man could die to free a nigger, why not let a nigger die in his place?

I ignored that. Because, you see, I didn't care if they wanted us to fight to get rid of us or to welcome us as equals. I simply felt that it was my war too. It had become a war to free my people. I thought of Pa and Ma. I thought of the preacher, still most likely living on that damned farm with that monster Ben lording over him. I thought of all the people I'd seen on the road heading north, singing songs of freedom, dreaming of freedom, wanting nothing more out of life than to be left alone, to live in peace. To never have to be afraid of another man, to never wake up one morning and find that their son, their daughter, their husband, wife, father or mother was being torn from their arms and sold away. I'd lost everything to slavery—my family, my friends and, down deep, a respect for myself that I was now only starting to rediscover.

That was worth fighting for, and worth dying for.

And then at last came the day.

It was getting into the middle of December of 1863. Jim and I went to church and Pastor White came in and his eyes were all aglowing. He got up into the pulpit and we could see he was excited and told us to hold off on our singing for a minute because he had an announcement to make.

"I've just received a letter," he said, "from Governor Morton of Indiana. It states that on December twenty-fourth, 1863, a recruiting office will open in this church to form up Indiana's first black regiment to fight in the war. My friends, our day to fight for our freedom has arrived!"

The tears started to stream down his face.

"I've prayed for this chance for over twenty years," he said, his voice shaking. "I ran away from slavery, a slavery right in the very capital city of this nation, named after Washington. When I left I knew I would never see my mother again. I fled to a foreign country, where I learned to read, to write and to preach the word of the Lord. I came back to my country, and I stand here to tell you that this is my country, and I am here to help in the fight of freedom for my brothers and sisters. I've prayed that there would come a day when black men of this country could stand together with white men and forever break the chains of slavery. I want you all to know that I have volunteered to serve as a private. God bless the cause of the Union and freedom."

We all came to our feet, shouting and cheering. Pastor White came down from his pulpit and we gathered around him and started to sing.

My chance had come at last.

Chapter 4

★　　★　　★

It was a chilly, blustery morning, a couple of days before Christmas of 1863. Right after church we went to Mr. Speed and told him what we intended to do. He sat us down in his little office, even gave us cups of coffee since it was so cold outside, and tried to talk us out of it.

"This damned war's killed my brother, crippled a cousin, and there's not a home in the North that's not suffered from it," he said sadly. "I'm telling you boys that there's a lot of folks that don't like the idea of colored soldiers; some say that the Fifty-fourth didn't prove anything since it still lost the fight."

"But they died like men," I said quietly.

"Son, just going out to get yourself killed ain't gonna prove nothing," Mr. Speed snapped. "It ain't gonna help you or your people, it ain't gonna end this war one day sooner, and you'll get yourself shoveled into some unmarked grave like my brother did."

He said the words coldly, almost spitting them out.

"I'm trying to tell you that it just won't make any difference one way or the other whether you join up or not. Some folks say that the colored soldiers will just stay in the rear. You'll stand around guarding some forgotten crossroads until hell freezes over. Others say we should use you up at the front and save the lives of white soldiers. Either way you'll come out on the short end of it."

"Mr. Speed, you've been mighty fine to my cousin and me," Jim said softly, "and we're beholden to you for it. But Sam here is afire to go, and I guess I am too. It might not mean anything to anyone else, but it means something in here," and he pointed to where his heart was.

Jim was never one much for talking. I think I did most all of it for both of us, but when he did speak, his words hit with a truth that couldn't be argued with.

Mr. Speed nodded sadly and told us to take the day off to go see if we could join.

So the following morning there we were in front of the church. There were hundreds of black folks out on the street that day, all of us bundled up against the cold wind. It was quite the circus, people talking, laughing, saying how now that black soldiers were getting into the war we'd lick the secess for sure. I saw one fellow pull his shirt off and show his scars, saying that when he got back down into Georgia he was going to find his old master and box his ears off.

They opened up the doors at last and there we were on a long line to go in and sign up. I got nervous for two reasons. The first was that we were far back in the line and I was afraid that they'd sign up everyone in front of us and we'd get left behind. The second fear was that they wouldn't let me join up.

You see, I was around fourteen then and wasn't all that big for my age. Now, I'd heard how they were going to ask me about my age and that if I didn't say eighteen they wouldn't let me join. I worried over that until I heard how a lot of white boys, when they went to join, would write the number eighteen on a piece of paper and put it inside their shoe. When the recruiting sergeant asked them their age they could then say, "I'm over eighteen," and they wouldn't be committing the sin of lying, especially in a church. So that's what I did.

We slowly made our way up the steps and fellows that had gone in ahead of us started to come out. Some looked really proud, and strutted about, saying they were going to be soldiers, while others, and this was most of them, came out looking like they'd been beaten; their heads were down and some were cursing, a few were even crying, they were so upset because they hadn't been taken.

We got into the church at last and it was awfully warm in there. I started to sweat and pulled off the raggy, old jacket I was wearing. I had on the only half-decent shirt that I owned, which Auntie Hubbard, the woman who ran our boardinghouse, had specially washed for me and even patched up when I told her I was going to join up.

We went up to the front where the pulpit was and I felt really embarrassed because there was a line of fellows and they had their shirts off and some had their pants down while a doctor walked around them, and poked and listened to their chests. We went up to a table and this mean-looking sergeant stared up at Jim, who was ahead of me. Behind him stood Pastor White.

"What's your name, son?"

"Jim Washburn."

"Place of birth?"

"I think it must be Kentucky."

"Parents living?"

"They's dead."

"How old are you?"

"Eighteen."

He looked at Jim and I could see a flicker of approval in his eyes. Jim was powerfully built by now; a year of good food and hard work had made his arms and shoulders look like chiseled rock.

"Take off your clothes and let the doc look at you."

Well, the doc was none other than Reverend Revel, who

was also a doctor. Now that got me real nervous because not only was I planning to lie, but I was planning to lie in my own church and right in front of my own pastor.

Jim felt really shy but did as he was told. Doctor Revel put his head up against Jim's chest and told him to breathe. Then he had him open his mouth and looked at his tongue and teeth. Finally he had him read some letters written on the wall, which Jim stumbled through.

"He'll do," Revel said, and the sergeant smiled and told Jim to go to the next table.

I stepped up to the sergeant, who looked at me and shook his head.

"Don't tell me, you're over eighteen, right?"

"That's right, sir," I said, trying to keep the trembling out of my voice.

I was too ashamed to look over at Pastors White and Revel, who I knew were staring straight at me. I guess I really started to break into a sweat right then. I heard Reverend White cough really loud, like he was an actor on the stage, and the sergeant looked back at him. The sergeant turned then and looked back at me.

"Sonny, go home and come back in two or three years."

"I'm over eighteen and I want to go fight the secess," I blurted out, trying to make my voice sound low and keep the trembling out of it. "Please don't send me away 'cause I'll follow you all the way down to where the war is even if you won't let me join."

The sergeant actually smiled, which I came to learn was mighty rare.

"Sonny, go home."

"If he don't go, I don't go," Jim said quietly.

"You his brother?" the sergeant asked.

"No, his cousin, but I promised his ma I'd look after him.

We's the only family we've got for each other and if he don't go, I ain't goin' either."

The sergeant sighed and looked Jim over almost with the same look the old slave buyers would give. The sergeant turned around again to look at White and Revel.

"You know this boy?" the sergeant asked.

"He's one of my flock," Revel said.

Reverend White looked at me real close and I didn't drop my eyes but I stared straight at him. I guess something happened between us at that moment, maybe he saw himself in me. The tiniest of smiles flickered across Reverend White's face.

"I guess Sam here just looks a bit short for his age, Sergeant. Maybe he is over eighteen at that."

With that Pastor White winked at me like we had a secret together which we'd always keep.

"Boy, can you play a drum?" the sergeant asked, looking back at me and smiling as well.

"Sure, I can," I said, knowing it was a lie but figuring it'd be easy to learn.

"Then you're a drummer boy; check him over, Doc, and make sure he passes."

I took my clothes off and stepped before Doctor Revel, the pastor of my church. The same as with Reverend White, I looked him straight in the eyes. I could see the anguish in his gaze. He knew my passion, knew what I desired, but I guess he sensed as well that if he nodded his head and said yes, he might be sending me to my death.

"I want this more than anything in the world, Parson," I whispered. "You've told us our faith is worth dyin' for. Well, Parson, freedom is worth dyin' for as well."

I could see tears clouding his eyes, and his gaze dropped.

"Sergeant, this one looks fine to me," he whispered.

And then he did something I'll never forget. He leaned over and kissed me lightly on the cheek, the way a father would kiss his son.

"God be with you, son," he whispered, and it was a hard fight for me not to start crying as well.

I picked up my clothes and moved to one side. I heard a chuckle and turned. It was the sergeant, and he was holding up a slip of paper.

"Sonny, this fell out of your shoe," he said with a grin and I saw he was holding the piece of paper with the number eighteen written on it. For a second I thought they were going to throw me out. Revel, the sergeant and the pastor all started to laugh, though, and everyone else on the line did too.

We went up to the next table, where they wrote down our names on an official-looking piece of paper and asked me if I could write. I told them I could and the man handed me a pen and, real careful-like, I wrote my name where he showed me to—"Samuel Washburn." Next they had Jim and me raise our hands and swear an oath. It was the most solemn moment of my life. Here were all these white officers and sergeants, a big American flag behind them, all of them looking at us. I followed the words promising to uphold and defend the State of Indiana, to obey my officers and to defend the Constitution of the United States of America.

Now that I look back upon it, it was a moment that set me down a path to my life which I never expected possible. If I'd gone back out that door, if Jim hadn't called their bluff, how different it'd all be now, both for him and for me. But we didn't. I'd have to say that there's a whole hell of a lot that maybe I didn't get because I was born a slave, and with the war now long gone there's a lot I still don't have. But on the other side there's a lot I do have that I'd never thought I'd get, and maybe, just maybe my grandson's grandson might have just as much as anyone else, white or black. But at least it was a start.

What makes me sad, though, when I think of it all, is that it sent Jim down a certain path as well.

We got done with the swearing-in part and I felt as if my heart would burst with pride. I thought we would go out the back door, get the blue Yankee suits, a gun, and take the next train down to secess land. I hoped we'd march right back down through Perryville. Why, wouldn't old Preacher just jump for joy to see us, I imagined, and wouldn't that Ben Washburn turn tail and run like the coward he was?

But instead a sergeant just handed us a piece of paper and told us to be at the courthouse at three o'clock and that was it. As we started for the door Pastor White came up to us and shook our hands.

"I'm proud of both you boys, mighty proud."

"Thanks for helpin' Sam to get in," Jim said with a smile.

"We need men like the two of you, hundreds of thousands of men for the work that's got to be done."

He shook our hands again and then went back to watch the next candidate, Ransom Felton, whose daughter Jim was sweet on, getting checked over by the sergeant.

We wandered back outside. Jim and I both stuck our chests out and strutted down the stairs and felt like just everyone was looking at us and admiring us.

There were a couple of white folks standing at the edge of the crowd, though, and funny as it might seem I thought they'd treat us with some respect. But they didn't.

"Hey, nigger, you a soldier now?" one of them asked, and the other one laughed.

Jim and I tried to ignore them but they pressed in a bit around us.

"Hey, boy, I'm talkin' to you," one said.

"Yes, we's soldiers now," Jim said quietly, and they started to laugh.

"How much they paying you, nigger?"

"Didn't need to pay us anything, we volunteered," I said and that started them to laughing again.

"Hell, boy, they's paying white men five hundred dollars' bounty to join up now and you stupid niggers are doin' it for free."

That got me mad. I'd heard about the bounty and couldn't understand it at all. Yes, we did get paid a hundred dollars after we were in camp, money I gave to Miss Latimer to hold until I came home, but that wasn't the reason why I had joined.

"I don't need to get paid to see my people free," I said coldly.

"Well, hell, better you niggers get killed than a white man." One of them laughed and they turned and walked away.

I wanted to say something but Jim put his hand on my shoulder and turned me away. I've learned long ago that there are too many folks like that in this world, white and black. I thought of the soldiers we met on the road when we were escaping. They'd joined the army when the war started, volunteered like we did, without thought of pay. And then there were others, like those fellas that laughed at us and called us stupid and then walked away, leaving someone else to do their fighting and their dying for them. Maybe we were stupid; I thought that more than once when I finally saw the fields of dead. But then again, when I shave each morning I still can look straight into the mirror and not sideways, the way I think those two must have felt at times.

We headed back to Auntie Hubbard's place and she met us at the door. She fell into crying when we told her we were in the army and she set us a big special meal of hotcakes with real syrup and coffee. Folks came in from all up and down the street and shook our hands, saying how proud they were that there were going to be real colored soldiers now, right from where they lived. Many of them were runaways like ourselves and they all started telling us where they were from again and making us promise that if we ever got near there, to tell their friends and families they were safe up north.

We said our good-byes and Auntie said she'd look after what few things we had and keep them safe till we came back. She kissed us both, hid her face in her apron and ran back into the kitchen.

Next we went over to see Mr. Speed. He got really quiet for a while and blew his nose noisily. He gave each of us a silver dollar and told us that if we needed work after the war to come see him, since the trains would always need more wood.

Jim went over to Ransom Felton's house, not so much to see Ransom, who we found out was accepted like us, but rather to see his daughter Mary. I left Jim there and went down the street to where the Quaker school was. I slipped in and Miss Latimer saw me standing in the back of the room.

The class of little ones got really quiet. Miss Latimer smiled and asked why I was there during the day and not at work.

I told her I was joining the army and came to say good-bye and to thank her. Well, she started to cry and that made me really uncomfortable, having a white woman crying over me like that. She wiped the tears from her eyes, went to the front of the room and opened up her desk. She got out two small books and told me to come up. She handed me the books and told me they were mine. One was a sixth-form McGuffey Reader, and the other one was the Bible.

I couldn't speak, I was so taken aback. Books for the school were mighty scarce and we weren't allowed to take them home and now for the first time in my life I had two of them.

Then the biggest shock of all was when she kissed me on the forehead and said she'd pray for me every night till I came home. I'm not ashamed to admit that I got a bit choked up and couldn't speak. It wasn't how I figured a soldier should act when going away. But I was only fourteen and the way she said "come home" just hit me hard. I could almost see my ma standing there instead of her. And the fact that it was a white woman crying over me as well just took me aback. She was one of the kindest women I'd ever known. It was awfully hard saying good-bye, harder than I ever imagined possible.

I met Jim back at Ransom's and Mary was sobbing, kissing him and saying that she'd wait for him and they would get married when he came back home. Ransom seemed pleased with this but Mary's ma was awfully upset and I think she was glad when we were back out on the street and heading downtown to the courthouse, with Ransom saying he'd be along shortly.

We got there just before three and there was near on to a hundred men waiting.

We were all excited and I recognized some of them. Natt Gibbs and Bill Bass both worked down at the railyard and they were glad to see us, as were George Walker and Alfred Mason, who both belonged to the same church we did. Natt was not much bigger than me and nearly died of the typhoid like I had and I was surprised he got in. Bill was like Jim, powerfully strong, with a nasty scar on his arm which he said was a knife wound from when he ran away, though Alfred told us he got it when he tripped and fell down a flight of stairs and the bottle in his pocket broke.

Everyone was all excited, laughing and talking, with kinfolk gathered round, some of them crying. The courthouse bell rang three, and from out of the courthouse came a really fine-looking officer, all decked out with fancy gold braid, and behind him came four sergeants, one of them being the fellow that let me sneak in.

They told us to get quiet and then with some fussing and cursing got us to stand in a column with four men in each line. They told us we were going to walk to the state fairgrounds, where the mustering camp and drill fields were. They even had a drummer to march us along and I looked over at him curiously. Now, I had wanted to join to carry a gun; I wanted to fight. But if they wouldn't let me carry a gun, at least I could beat on the drum for starters and maybe later on, when I grew a bit, I'd get a gun. So this drummer started into beating and it put a chill down my spine and the sergeant told us to start walking. Everyone was shouting good-bye and we felt like real heroes, figuring we'd be in the war in no time.

It sounds kind of foolish now, but we didn't get out of town for another four whole months.

Chapter 5

★　★　★

Well, it was a good five-mile walk up to the fairgrounds, now called Camp Fremont, which served as a depot and training ground for the new soldiers going into the army. The little march we took drew a lot of stares and comments from people who saw us. Some laughed, some said mighty nasty things, and some even waved and cheered, which made us smile and wave in return. We even sang a bit, not the regular songs of the army but our own songs, like "Go Down, Moses," "Follow the Drinkin' Gourd," and other tunes we'd sung quietly, late at night, back home in the South when we dreamed of freedom.

We reached the fairgrounds outside of town and it was getting on towards evening and a cold wind was blowing. We were taken to our barracks, which were nothing more than a bunch of boards slapped together, but each of them had a real woodstove inside, and compared with some of the places we'd lived in, they were actually better than most.

I think that was one of the real advantages we had, and would always have over white soldiers in that war. Most of the white soldiers came from comfortable homes, ate good food and maybe didn't even work with their hands. But for us colored soldiers it was different. Many of us were born in slavery, worked from before dawn till after dark under the threat of the lash, and thought ourselves really lucky if there was a bit of old chewy pork in one of our meals. We lived in shacks that were crawling with bugs and at best had a smoky fireplace for a little warmth in winter. We went barefoot near to year-round and dressed in thrown-off rags that barely covered us.

The army was damn near to heaven itself in comparison. If we walked twenty miles at drill it was no worse than a hard day's work in the fields. We were given fine wool uniforms and real shoes, and many of the men had never had shoes in their life. And the food—well, this might make many an old soldier laugh but I tell you the food was wonderful, far better than what we were used to. Hardtack, salt pork and real coffee was a king's meal compared to what a slave usually eats. The only problem with all of this was you had people trying to kill you.

So we were shown into our barracks, which had real cots with blankets on them. Next we were taken to the quartermaster and lined up. We went into his room wearing rags and each of us came out with the best Christmas gift in the world—a blue Yankee uniform.

Now, he just sort of threw the uniforms at us and they really didn't fit. My trousers were so long that I had to roll them halfway to my knees to keep from tripping and you could darned near fit a second person in around the waist. The sleeves on the jacket came down past my fingertips, while Jim seemed like he was near ready to burst out of his. The shoes were really heavy, with no left or right foot in them. The sergeant said we should soak them first in water and then walk around in them and they'd soon fit. Our belts were made of black leather and the buckle was shiny brass with *U.S.* stamped on it. They even gave us fine white linen shirts, gray wool socks, and underwear, something I'd never worn in my life. We were all laughing and shouting like little children on

Christmas morning. I kept my shirt that Auntie Hubbard patched, but what was left of my shoes and my trousers I just threw away, since they were all gone to holes anyhow.

Next we were taken to a dining hall and they served out a Christmas meal to us: smoked ham, sweet potatoes, pickled beets, fresh coffee and apple pie. I ate till I thought I'd burst and I thought that this army business was just fine and you'd have to be a fool not to love it.

I soon learned how much of a fool I truly was. I was too innocent to even think that for most of the fellows there, it would be the last Christmas dinner they'd ever know.

Christmas Day was really easy and we just sort of lay around, eating, spinning yarns and thinking we were mighty fine fellows. The following morning, at six o'clock, we found out that the party was over.

The white sergeant, whose name was McClousky, the one who'd let me sign up, came storming into our barracks swearing and yelling, screaming at us to get out of bed and get dressed.

The way he was acting I thought the war had come straight to Indianapolis and that maybe there were Rebel raiders heading our way.

We scrambled out of the barracks and I thought my breath was going to freeze in my lungs, it was so cold. He made us line up and already I was starting to shiver.

"You are the dumbest, ugliest-looking sons of bitches I've ever laid my eyes on," he roared. "How the hell our country's ever gotten itself into this fix of letting a bunch of ignorant idiots like you into my army is beyond me."

That was just for starters and he screamed at us for ten or fifteen minutes. Then he told us all to go back inside to straighten up our cots. We ran back in like he told us to, grateful to get out of the cold, but he followed us in, cursing and yelling. He stopped in front of one fellow, James Barnes, who was by far the biggest man in our company, and could even lick Jim, and started into cussing at him. James started to look really angry but said nothing.

"I bet you think you can lick me, boy," the sergeant finally growled.

James looked a bit nervous at this.

"What's the matter, you afraid to try me, boy?"

"Boss, I ain't got no cause to go fightin' with a white man," he said quietly, but you could see he was getting mighty angry.

"Come on, boy, what's the matter, you afraid? I'll even let you take first swing, and if you lick me I won't say a word."

James looked around at us and we all got real quiet.

"Come on, boy, try me," and he pushed him slightly.

Well, James's fist just shot out like lightning, but there wasn't anyone there for it to connect with. The sergeant just stepped to one side, and as quick as a striking snake, his foot went up into James's gut and then a fist connected with his jaw. James got a really strange look in his eyes, like they were going to pop out, and he just doubled over and hit the floor.

The sergeant looked around the room.

"Anyone else wanna try?"

We were silent as a graveyard.

He reached down and helped James back up.

"No shame in it, boy. No shame in it. You're acting corporal now."

James nodded, but didn't have much to say about how he got his promotion.

After that we were run over to the dining hall for a breakfast of oatmeal mush with a little pork fat mixed in and then back out to a drill field.

The sun was just starting to come up, and the field was all covered with a heavy frost that crunched under our feet. Now, as for my feet, they were already getting sore. It wasn't so much that the shoes were breaking in to fit me, rather it was my feet were starting to break in to fitting them.

"Now, when we march we start off with out left foot, like this," the sergeant roared and he showed us.

"Now, when I say 'forward march,' start with your left foot.

"Forward march!"

We all stepped off and he started into screaming for us to stop. He did it four or five times and I thought he was going to burst a blood vessel, his face was so purple.

"How many of you benighted bastards don't know which is your left foot?"

A fair number of men raised their hands. He lowered his head, shaking it, and saying things that I'd never heard before but figured were some fine and powerful curses.

The sergeant walked us over to a stable, went in and came out with a handful of hay and straw. He walked down the line and gave each of us a piece of hay and straw, and then had us tuck the hay into our left shoe and the straw into our right shoe.

"Now, when I say 'hay foot,' I mean your left foot, do you understand me?

"Get ready now. Forward march! Hay foot, straw foot, hay foot, straw foot."

A lot of the boys still had some trouble with it, but by the middle of the day he had us doing tolerably well so that we all started off with the correct foot. To this day, though, when I see a piece of hay, it almost starts my left foot to twitching a bit.

Next he got us to line up in what was called a column of fours, which was four men in a line, one line behind the other, and started us into marching. The hard part came when we got across that field and it came time for us to make a right turn to the straw foot side, but still stay in the column. It all fell apart and we all got tangled up, some of the fellows turning left, while others immediately turned even though their line wasn't anywhere near the place where they were supposed to turn. I had a big shoe print on my backside where the sergeant kicked me back into place. Everything was starting to get muddy since the sun was warm and melting the frost.

By the late part of the afternoon I felt like my feet were bleeding, and it turned out they were, with some of the blistering breaking open. A couple of the men, after a short rest break, tried to return to the marching with their shoes off, but he screamed and yelled some more, saying we had to wear the shoes and made the men put them back on.

When we finally went back to the barracks after dark I thought my legs were going to fall off me, my feet hurt so much. Jim, however, didn't have a word of complaint. He said this army business was a hell of a lot easier than clearing rocks from a field or pulling tree stumps and most of the other men agreed with him.

After supper I sat down with my McGuffey Reader and started into studying. Several of the men gathered round and asked me if I could read and write. Now, I wasn't all that good yet but I was proud to show them that I could write my name and before I knew it, I was volunteered into being a teacher, a job I had for the rest of the time I was in the army.

So our days went, getting up every morning before dawn to drill in fair weather or foul, snow or rain, warm or freezing cold. We drilled, and then we drilled, and then we drilled some more, and then after that they threw in a little more drill, and then after that yet some more drill, finishing up with a bit of extra drill thrown in.

We learned how to march in a column and to turn left, right and about. That was the easy stuff. Next they started teaching us marching like we'd do in battle. We had to be able to go from a marching column and with a couple of steps shake it out into a battle line two men deep and fifty men long.

Then after we got that they started into showing us how to

march in a battle line, keeping it straight and then being able
to turn it one way or the other, telling us we'd never know
when the Rebs might pop up on what was called our flank and
we'd have to face them in this new direction. After we got it all
down in regular marching time they started into making us do
it at the double-quick march and finally at a full run.

Well, my shoes finally came to fit my feet, or maybe it was
the other way around, and what with the army food we were
eating I started to put on weight and even filled out a bit,
though I could tell I'd never get as big as Jim.

Every couple of weeks another company of new recruits
for our regiment would come marching into camp. We'd look
at them and laugh, telling them how'd they'd be sorry and
wondering if we ever looked as raggedy and stupid as they did.
Pastor White came in with D Company and he fell right into
the work. I heard they offered him a chance to be a sergeant,
which was the highest rank a black man could hold back then,
but he refused, saying he wanted to be just like the rest of his
flock. He seemed to be everywhere, encouraging men who got
discouraged, telling jokes to cheer us up and leading us in
prayer services every night. I was proud to be in the same regiment with him and thought he was the finest soldier and one
of the two finest preachers I ever knew.

The new companies were soon out on the drill field with
us. Pretty soon the sergeants had us marching with two, three
and four companies together so that we could go from a column of fours into a battalion front battle line, which means five
companies standing in one long line of men two deep, the line
stretching for over a hundred yards. Then they'd have us
march across the field. It was a sight to behold and set your
blood to pumping, what with everyone marching and the
tramping of our feet. From there we might have to go into what
was called a column of companies, which meant that we as
A Company lined up first, fifty men to the first rank and fifty to

the second. Behind us then came companies B and C and so on. The sergeant said this was one of the formations we might use when we were charging Rebel trenches, and he was quick to point out that being that we were A Company, we'd have the honor of being right up front.

After a couple of months they started giving stripes to some of us. James Barnes got to be a corporal for real. Ransom Felton, whose daughter Jim was stuck on, got to be our first sergeant. He was a slight fellow, not much taller than myself, and I'd be willing to bet a month's pay that James could have knocked Ransom's head off with a single blow. But being a sergeant doesn't mean you have to be the strongest. Ransom was a free-man long before the war and even owned a small carpentry shop. He was a quiet fellow, could read, and his voice was deep and smooth; at church service you could always hear it leading the songs.

He just sort of seemed like a father somehow, a bit older than the rest of us. He called most of us "son" and it seemed like he really meant it, like he was a father looking out for us. After the day's drill was done he'd go up to fellows who had a hard time and take them out behind the barracks. He'd practice with them, smiling and patting them on the back when they finally did it right. You just wanted to make Sergeant Felton proud of you.

Every night, when he wasn't out practicing with somebody, he'd sit in the corner of the barracks studying a book by someone named Hardee, which explained how all the army drills were supposed to be done. Pretty soon McClousky started to step aside and let Ransom run our drills. He was really good at it and we were proud that we had a black man as our leader.

Francis Jones, who was a runaway from Tennessee, was our sergeant under Ransom. He was a woodcutter the way Jim and I had been, and had a terrible-looking scar on his face from where a double-bladed ax had bounced back off a knot and cut

him. I guess you could say he was the tough fighter of the company, but he wasn't a bully, and when he took a fellow out for
thrashing it was because there was no other way. Francis and
Ransom worked together as a team, the one talking softly, the
other ready to move if a fellow didn't get into line after the soft
talking.

Though Garland White had enlisted as a private, he was finally convinced by everyone to accept the rank of regimental
sergeant-major.

His energy and enthusiasm were boundless. During the
day he could be the toughest of sergeants, pacing from one end
of the drill field to the other. If a man wasn't doing his job, he
could be tougher than McClousky, his voice booming across
the parade ground.

"You think the secess will take pity on you when the bullets are flying and men are dying all around you? Now get back
in line and prove what kind of man you are!"

At night he was, again, the parson tending to his flock.
He'd hold prayer services, write letters for those who couldn't
write and have a gentle word for those who were homesick.
He encouraged a number of men to take reading lessons from
me, and I'd sometimes have twenty men or more sitting
around me. Now I wasn't all that good at it yet; I'd stumble
over many a word, but when I did, Garland would be standing
there, smiling, gently correcting me and then leaving me to my
task. I realize now it'd of been far easier for him to do the
teaching himself, but he wanted me to learn even as I taught
and also to be respected by the men I would go into battle
with.

By the beginning of February we had five companies of
soldiers mustered in. When they drilled us all together it was a
sight to behold, five hundred men all dressed in the dark blue
jackets and sky-blue trousers of the Yankee army. We'd move
across the drill field like a wave, the thunder of our feet pound-

ing out the rhythm of the march, shouted commands echoing against the barracks buildings.

Just about that time they finally issued us our muskets and that was a day of celebration. We were taken down to a warehouse, lined up, and each of our five hundred men was handed a brand-new, shiny Springfield rifled musket. I looked on, just filled with envy, since as a drummer boy I wasn't going to get one.

Sergeant McClousky took our company out to a field and he showed us how the musket worked. First you had to tear open a paper cartridge with your teeth. Inside of the cartridge was a .58-caliber bullet, what we called a minié ball, and some gunpowder. You poured the powder down the barrel and then pushed the bullet down on top and threw the paper away. Next you pulled out your ramrod and pushed it all straight down to the bottom of the barrel. Then you brought the gun up, half cocked it and took out a tiny, little copper percussion cap from a pouch on your belt and put it on the nipple just below the hammer. Then you cocked it all the way back, aimed the gun and fired.

The sergeant fired a shot and it was so loud it made me jump. For a second I remembered back to when Ben Washburn had that gun aimed at my face and it went off. The sergeant allowed each of the men to fire half a dozen times and Jim actually hit the target, which was a big picture of the secess president, Jefferson Davis.

They didn't get to fire their guns again for weeks after that, and instead had to learn all the drills of how to carry it and such. But after that Sergeant McClousky took us down to an open field and pretty soon the men were learning how to load and fire by volley, a hundred muskets going off at once, and some of the fellows got so good they could get off three aimed shots in a minute.

I wasn't left completely out, though. The day after everyone got their guns I was called over to a building with all the drummer boys from the other companies and we were each handed a brand-new drum and drumsticks. I felt so proud I thought I'd just burst. The drum was really pretty, with an eagle painted on its side, and in its beak the eagle was holding a long streamer that was painted red, white and blue.

They had a white drummer boy there and he was a friendly enough fellow who right away started into teaching us. We first learned how to hold our drumsticks. We must have been a funny sight, all standing around, grinning, laughing, dropping our sticks, but we finally started to get the hang of it. Off at the far end of the barracks room they had some other boys learning how to play fifes and the shrieking of them sent cold chills down your back, for they sounded like someone had set into strangling a bunch of canary birds. Outside they had some other boys with bugles and they sounded like a bunch of dying cows.

First we learned the slow roll, then the fast roll, then the long roll, which was the signal for a charge, and a whole bunch of other beats. When you were standing still it was easy enough to do after a couple of days, but the drum was rather big, and when you started into marching it'd bob up and down and you had to learn the rhythm of moving your hands up and down, keeping your arms rising and falling, and stay in step all at the same time.

We didn't just have to learn how to march and play, but also to listen for when orders were shouted, because we were expected to signal the orders by the drumbeat and then follow and turn, run, walk, turn around, go left, go right and stand still all at the same time. I felt a deep responsibility with all of this, because if I didn't do it right, and made a terrible mistake, like beating the signal for retreat when I should beat the charge, I could lose a whole battle in no time flat all by myself.

After a week or so of practicing they let us start marching

with the soldiers again out on the drill field and everyone just grinned with delight. The beating of my drum made the marching easier and made everyone feel like soldiers. Why, the first morning I got so puffed up with pride, being at the head of the column next to Sergeant McClousky, that when he shouted out for the column to go into line and turn left, I just kept on going straight ahead, listening to my drum beat away, figuring how everyone was just following me.

I woke up when I caught his foot right in my backside. He started hollering and cussing at me and the men was going every which way, with half turning left and the other half still following me and everyone all knotted up with confusion. He cussed me out something fierce, said I was a lunkhead of a little black fool, cussed me so hard that everyone else in the company just started to laugh and I was darned near set to cry, I was so ashamed. I never made that mistake again.

By the end of the day I started to feel a bit funny. My throat felt all tight and I started into sweating and then to shaking. I thought at first maybe the sergeant had kicked me so hard that he'd broken something inside. When it came to dinnertime I just didn't want to eat and the dining hall felt all tight and too crowded.

Jim kept looking at me and saying I was getting sick but I told him it was nothing. But it *was* something and by the next morning I was so sick I wanted to just roll over and die. I got these nasty-looking rashes all over me, and a funny, spotted color broke out all over my tongue. The rashes started to break and this waterlike stuff ran out of the little sores. Doctor Revel came in to look at me, said I had the measles, and for that matter so did three other fellas in my company, and near to thirty in the other companies.

The measles just ran through us like wildfire. Darned near half the company got sick with it and we just lay in our cots all day, groaning and sweating.

Four days after I caught it George Hays, who joined when I did, came down with an even worse dose. He started raving and talking crazy and they had to put a rope over him to keep him in his cot. He started to talk funny, saying his wife's name over and over again like she was there. Now, we all knew his wife was dead, having died when trying to have a baby, and I heard some of the men whispering that his wife had come to take him home to Jesus. Just before dawn he let out a cry and then got really still. I got scared when I saw the doctor come in and then have them carry George out with a blanket over his face. For days afterwards I was terrified that they'd finally come and put a blanket over my face as well.

George wasn't the only one to die of the measles. Near to ten other men died as well and that seemed to be only the start of it. Four men, including Leander Overman, who was only a year older than me, died of the galloping consumption and then a whole bunch of the men got a bad dose of the two steps, which killed half a dozen more. Seemed like we were all either coughing, groaning, running to the outhouse or throwing up. I heard the white sergeants say that whenever a new regiment formed up, near everybody got sick and a whole bunch would up and die. It was part of being in the army.

It took me a couple of weeks to get over it, and before I was fully well there was a scare when one of the men turned up with nasty pox marks on his face. Right away Revel came rushing in, we all had to take the smallpox inoculation, and for several days after that the entire regiment felt poorly and half a dozen men came down with bad cases of it. One of them got a terrible infection in his arm from the inoculation and for a while there, the doc worried that he might have to cut it clean off.

I was starting to see that getting sick in the army was maybe even more dangerous than getting shot at.

March was the sick time and from then on, there was always ten or twenty men in the regiment down with something or other. I gradually got better. For the first couple of days that I went out to drill I felt light-headed and the sergeant would look over at me and in an almost kindly voice tell me to go back to bed and rest some. I was finally able to stick through a day, though, and knew I was on the mend.

There started to be a touch of spring in the air. On the edge of the drill field we could see tufts of green shooting up. Robins would fly by and the air was filled with warmth so that you felt yourself coming alive again after a long, cold winter of chills and sickness. Quite a few fellows had died during the winter and a couple of dozen more just decided they didn't want army life anymore and ran off. We were ashamed of them because a lot of white folks had said that black soldiers would never stand it. Sergeant McClousky finally told us not to fret over it, saying that the regiment was better off without those kind anyhow, and when compared to a lot of white regiments being recruited now, where near to half the men ran off, we were doing just fine.

We knew things were stirring. We were starting to look darned good as soldiers and even the white sergeants said so, saying we were the easiest troops they'd ever drilled into shape. A couple of them, who obviously did not like colored folks, and said so right up front back in December, were now singing a different song and saying we just might be all right when we finally got into the fight.

Our own colored sergeants and corporals started taking over things more and more and that made us feel really proud. Recruiting for new soldiers, though, had fallen off considerably. The regiment was supposed to have a thousand men in it but so far we had only five companies of a hundred each, but then in late March a sixth company came in. Near to every able-bodied black man in Indiana had joined up. There were a lot more who tried but were turned down. We were anxious to get going. The newspapers, which I read aloud each night to the men, were full of stories of how, with the coming of spring, the big battles that would end the war would soon be fought out. Most of the papers were predicting that by the end of May it'd all be over.

We weren't sure where we were going yet. Some folks said we'd wind up going down to Louisiana, where there were a whole bunch of colored regiments. Others figured on the coast of South Carolina, where the famous old 54th Massachusetts was fighting, while others said we'd wind up going east to fight under Grant and the Army of the Potomac, which was tangling with Robert E. Lee.

Our white officers started to show up. You see, not until near into the end of the war did they allow black soldiers to be officers. Captain McHenry took over as commander of our company and he came from a Pennsylvania regiment. He was a tall, slender man who wore spectacles, his face all covered with freckles. I liked him from the start. He could be as tough as hickory wood but was always fair. I was used to hearing white folks calling us niggers, and a lot worse, but he never used that word. He called us his men and treated us fairly.

He was joined by Lieutenant Grant from an Indiana regiment. He was short, with a bushy black beard and heavy eyebrows that seemed to run together. He always had a chew of tobacco in his cheek, a practice which I could never understand since I got sick the first time I tried it. He could cuss a blue streak better than any sergeant, which he'd been before joining us. He was a hard-driving man and we took to him as well, especially when we heard how he beat the stuffing out of a white officer from another regiment who said that we were a bunch of animals and cowards and would run in our first fight.

Finally, towards the end of April, we got the word that we were moving out and that additional companies of recruits would be sent out later to make us a full-size regiment. We were told to pack up our gear and to polish our equipment till it shined because we were going to parade through Indianapolis and down to the train station the following morning.

We were up half the night with the excitement and I rubbed linseed oil into my drum and buffed it till I could near see my face and my brass buckle looked almost silver. Come dawn we lined up on the drill field, six companies strong, our backs straight, our lines perfect.

Our white drill sergeants walked around us and spoke a bit, saying they were proud of us and knew we'd do well. They saluted our new white officers and then walked to the side of the field, replaced by our own black sergeants and corporals.

Our new commanding officer, Colonel Russell, rode out in front of us and said we were going to join the Army of the Potomac in Virginia. Now, that caused a stir. That was where the real thick of the fighting was going on. He said we'd be one of the first of the colored regiments to join that army, that a lot was resting on our shoulders and that he expected us to make him and the entire nation proud.

Orders were shouted down the line and we formed up into columns. I ran to the front of the column where all the drummers and fifers were lined up and we started off. We marched out of Camp Fremont, which had been our home for months, and our old sergeants were lined up, saluting us as we passed.

We started down the road towards town and as we got into the city it seemed like everyone was turned out, white and black, and all of them were joined in shouting and cheering for us.

We turned down onto Market Street, heading for the capitol building, our drums thundering, and stopped in front of the building where Governor Morton was standing.

We came to a halt and he looked out at us and we could see he was proud.

He gave us a short speech and then at the end of it he motioned for a group of black women to come up and join him. They were carrying two flags: one was the state flag of Indiana, the other one the flag of the United States of America. They were members of Revel's church and had sewn the flags for us. There in gold letters on both sides of each flag was the proud name: "28th Regiment, United States Colored Troops."

Morton took the flags and then Colonel Russell, with Sergeant Felton and Sergeant White, stepped forward to receive the flags. Russell said that we would carry the flags with honor, that they'd always be at the front of the battle and would never touch the ground or be taken by the Rebels.

We gave him three cheers and the whole square just echoed with people hollering. It sent chills down my spine. There in the crowd I saw Auntie Hubbard just waving away at me, and a bit behind her stood Mr. Speed and Miss Latimer, who looked at me so sadly.

The colonel got back on his horse and trotted out to the front of the column. Sergeant Felton carried one of the flags and Sergeant White took the other.

With a roll of my drum the entire regiment started forward again and the drum major called for "The Battle Hymn of the Republic." The fifers, who'd been practicing that tune for weeks, picked up the song. I rolled out the beat and behind me half a thousand men started into singing. The sound of the drums, the fifes and the voices echoed against the buildings, and the people lining the streets joined in.

We marched down the street, the voices of the men booming, mingling with the cheers, the tears and the shouts of the people waving farewell. Families came out of the crowd, rushing up to hug their husbands, sons, brothers and fathers one last time. I saw Mary running past me, her mother struggling to hold her back, and knew she was trying to reach Jim for one final kiss.

When we got to the last line of the song, "As He died to

make men holy, let us die to make men free," I felt like icy water had been poured down my back and I could hardly sing the words. All I could think of was my pa, my ma, the preacher, all those people we were on the road with, the white soldiers who'd helped us and most likely were long dead by now. The folks lining the street started to break down and cry as well and I sneaked a quick look back and saw the tears streaming down the faces of the black soldiers behind me.

It was the most awe-inspiring moment I had ever known in my short fourteen years of life. Two years ago I was a terrified runaway slave. Now I was part of a crusade to help set my people free. It was a moment that was worth dying for—a price more than one of us was soon to pay.

Chapter 6

★   ★   ★

Six days later our train pulled into Washington, the capital of the United States.

It'd been a long and slow ride out, some of it fun, especially when we were rolling along the first couple of days and the weather was fine. We were packed into boxcars and took to sitting on top of them, stretching out and watching the land pass by. The farms of Ohio were some of the richest I'd ever seen, neat and orderly, fences set out nice and straight, cows in the fields cropping on the first shoots of spring. Then the weather turned cold and rainy and it was just plain miserable. Some of the men were sick when we left and a couple of them died on the trip, while one soldier fell off the train and was crushed. It was a terrible thing to see, his body all torn apart by the wheels. It was a sight I'd get used to, but it made my stomach flip right over when I first looked at him.

Folks were friendly to us in Ohio, and in Dayton and Columbus they even gave us a real turnout of food at the station. But when we crossed into western Virginia and then into Maryland it wasn't quite so friendly anymore. When we got into Baltimore we had to march from one station to another to get on the final train to Washington. We all were told how Baltimore was a real secess town. Now the black folks, at the sight of us marching down the street, started cheering and pointing, following along, telling us how proud they were, but the white folks were downright sullen. One woman picked up a handful of mud and threw it at our flag and almost hit it.

I thought Colonel Russell was going to shoot her on the spot. He rode straight up to her. She looked up at him defiantly and said he was a nigger-loving Yankee. He said that since he was a gentlemen he couldn't even tell her what low sort of occupation he thought she practiced. He said she wasn't even fit to wipe the boots of his soldiers and if she didn't clear out that's exactly what he'd force her to do. We gave him a cheer for that and marched on while she slunk away into an alley.

We got into Washington late in the afternoon. The rail yard was just a madhouse. Dozens of trains were coming in and out, loaded down with soldiers and the machines of war. We passed a long line of flatcars packed from one end to the other with shiny, new bronze cannons which we soon learned were called Napoleons. They fired a twelve-pound cannonball, but at close range were packed with tin cans filled with sixty or seventy one-inch iron shot called canister. That turned the gun into a giant sawed-off shotgun that could cut down a whole company of men.

As we got off the train and lined up, I must say we caused quite a stir since colored regiments were still kind of new to the army, especially the one fighting in Virginia. We turned out onto Pennsylvania Avenue and started marching. There was no parade this time. Hundreds of regiments had been marching through Washington for over three years now, and though we caused a bit of a stir with being a colored regiment, most folks barely noticed us.

We were all eyes, though. Off to our left we saw the nearly completed dome of the Capitol building and the street was lined with tall trees. It was far and away the biggest city I'd ever seen in my life. We continued down the street and the colonel called for a song, "We Are Coming, Father Abraham."

I picked up the beat, the fifes started to shriek, our regiment commenced to singing and then straight ahead I saw a big white mansion. It was Lincoln's home and even as we sang the men started to point and shout. The song started to break down and the men began to chant.

"Father Abraham, Father Abraham!"

And then I couldn't believe my eyes, for there he was, coming out to stand on the front porch, a little fellow, who I reckoned was his son, standing beside him and holding his hand.

At the sight of him the regiment almost broke apart to swarm towards him; men were crying, shouting, taking off their hats, cheering. Colonel Russell turned his horse and looked back at us, his deep voice thundering for us to come to attention and march like soldiers.

We fell into line and continued on, but all eyes were turned towards him. When our flag went past, he put his hand over his heart and the boy saluted. He looked terribly old, as if bent down by a thousand years of woe and troubles. I always heard how he was such a tall man, but somehow I expected him to almost be a giant, sort of like the way I pictured Saint Peter might look standing by the gates of heaven. But he almost looked small, so burdened did he seem at that moment, a black shawl draped over his bony shoulders. I felt as if I knew what he was thinking as he watched us march by, that we were his soldiers, that he had set us free to go off and die. I think he was wondering how many of us would get safely home again when it was all over and that it would keep on going like that until either the secess gave up or we were all dead and gone into the dust.

I'll never forget the look on his face as long as I live: it was as if the pain of our entire country was caught inside his soul. The others seemed to catch it as well and our voices grew still. We marched past, the men saluting, looking grim and determined, wanting him to be as proud of us as much as we loved him in return.

We marched on into the twilight and crossed the bridge into Virginia.

An orderly met Colonel Russell as we marched through the town of Alexandria, which was on the other side of the Potomac River from Washington, and said he'd guide us to our camp. We all thought that we were heading straight on down to the Rapidan River, fifty miles south of Washington, where the Army of the Potomac was, and were really disappointed to hear that we would be held near Washington as reserve troops.

We were assigned to Camp Casey, which was built right on the land owned by General Robert E. Lee. His mansion was just over the hill, and when we were given a little free time, we often walked around it, but no one was let inside other than some general who had taken it over as his headquarters.

The land we were camped on is a sacred place today. You see it got turned into a cemetery for the boys who died in the war, and it's now called Arlington Cemetery. I understand our barracks are long gone, but the graves, well I pray that the graves will remain there forever, a reminder to all of the cost of war and the price of freedom.

The next four weeks were nothing but a repeat of our long months of drill back in Indianapolis. We weren't allowed even to go into Washington to take a look around because the colonel said that colored troops being so new, there was some worry that we might find ourselves having some trouble. Now, that really bothered a lot of us. Here we had the blue Yankee suits on, but we weren't allowed to go visiting the way white soldiers could. The colonel told us that soon enough, after we proved ourselves in battle, things would change.

I still have to smile at that promise. I guess it meant that we had to die before we would be respected. I had to comfort myself with the thought that though I hadn't taken the full step out of slavery, at least I'd taken a half step, and maybe with a few more small steps I'd get the rest of the way. I think it made all of us want to prove something all the more, that we were the equal of any soldiers, North or South, black or white.

The month of May was a hard one on us. News came back that the Army of the Potomac, with over a hundred thousand men, had moved down to attack the Rebs and cross the Rapidan River into secess territory just west of the town of Fredericksburg, which was about halfway between Washington and the Rebel capital of Richmond.

And then came the word of the terrible battles that were fought. First there was the Battle of the Wilderness, and near on to twenty thousand men were killed or wounded in two days of fighting. The army under Grant didn't turn tail and run, though, the way they had in the past. This Grant, everyone was saying, was a real fighter and would stand toe to toe with old Robert E. Lee and his Army of Northern Virginia until the secess gave up.

A couple of days after the Wilderness came the Battle of Spotslyvania, which dragged on for a couple of weeks and saw another twenty thousand men go down. Trains and boats started coming back into Alexandria loaded down with the wounded. Pretty soon the ground in front of General Lee's mansion was all torn up with hundreds and hundreds of new graves.

One day our company was detailed off to go down and help. It was horrible work. We dug graves one after the other, and as fast as a hole was finished a couple of men came up carrying a stretcher, the body covered in a blanket. He'd get lowered in, a parson would say a couple of words and then they'd fill the hole in. We dug hard all morning and then took a break from work to eat our noonday meal of hardtack and salt pork. I finished up early and went down to the road by Lee's mansion. There was a long line of bodies; some were lucky enough to have coffins, but a lot were just wrapped up in blankets. There was a sticky, sweet smell to the air that made my stomach feel weak. A couple of soldiers saw me staring. Laughing, they pulled a blanket back and told me to come look.

I don't think the soldier was any older than me. His face was a pale green color, his eyes still open and, by God, both his legs were gone above the knees. I started shaking and turning away. I got sick to my stomach and the soldiers laughed. Sergeant Felton came up and yelled at the two men, saying there was something wrong with them if they had to get their fun by picking on a drummer boy.

One of them said he wouldn't take such talk from a colored man. Sergeant Felton got really quiet, pointed to his sleeve, said he was a noncommissioned officer and, black or white, his rank better be respected. He then told the two men to either help out with the work or clear off. There was something in his voice that had a real power to it, for the two men turned and walked away.

I felt so proud of the sergeant and how he handled himself; it was the first time in my life I ever heard a black man order a white man and have it obeyed. I came to realize that in the army, it was the rank that was important and that the color of a man's skin shouldn't matter in the slightest. It gave me a real feeling of hope, somehow.

I went over to that dead boy and pulled the blanket back up over his face. I said a short prayer for him, hoping that he was happy in heaven and that his ma would somehow be comforted. Later that day I helped to dig the grave that he would sleep in.

It finally got into the end of May and the heat was as bad as anything I'd seen in Kentucky, and then on the afternoon of

May 29, we got word that we were moving at last to go join the big fight down south. Grant's army had lost so many men in the fighting during May that they were stripping every regiment they could spare out of Washington to help fill the ranks back out.

Lord, was there a sea of laughing faces, shouting and hollering when the colonel called us all together and gave us the word. The following morning we marched down to the docks and got aboard an old steamship, which pulled out into the Potomac. We crowded the decks, shouting and waving, eager to be off. There were a whole bunch of white regiments that were heading out as well on other boats and most of them didn't seem at all as happy as we were. I guess we had a lot more to prove and knew it.

As we went down the river we saw the home of General Washington up high on a bluff looking out over the river, and then we were told to stay belowdecks because secess bushwhackers were known to come down to the river and take potshots at anything that went by. Belowdecks it was hot and awful stuffy, but we weren't complaining, and for the rest of the day we sang and some of the others played cards.

Now, card playing was a regular and full-time sin with the army, as was drinking, cussing and a lot of other things. I hate to tell it but Jim was real good at card playing and by the time we got to our destination, at White House, Virginia, he'd won near on to a hundred dollars. Sergeant White would wander around and when anyone saw him coming they'd quick hide the cards and whatever bottles of whiskey might be around. He'd come by and smile, say hello to everyone and then keep on going, and then the cards and whiskey would come out again. When I think about it now, I guess we weren't fooling him at all. He was a good parson and knew when it was time to preach and when it was time to let soldiers be soldiers.

It was early the following morning when our ship finally

docked at the town of West Point, Virginia, which was on the York River east of Richmond. West Point was really important to the army just then because they were fighting off by Richmond, about thirty miles away, and the supply ships would come down the Potomac River and then back up the York, bringing the food and equipment that the army needed.

When we got there, way off in the distance we heard a steady rolling thunder. Some of the fellas, myself included, thought it was a thunderstorm, which was strange since the sky was clear blue, but Lieutenant Grant said that it was the sound of battle and it sounded like an awfully big one.

That got us excited but at the same time we started to look at each other. We weren't told anything of what was going on but we commenced into marching, heading straight west towards the thunder. It was a terribly hot day, the sun just beating down on us. You have to remember that we were wearing heavy wool uniforms, wool jackets, wool pants, wool socks, and carrying over forty pounds of equipment. I didn't have to carry a gun or ammunition, but the drum was heavy enough and when playing it while walking it'd bang against my leg, and with all the sweating my leg was chafed by the wool.

The road was dry as a bone, and that red Virginia clay soil was all beat to a dust as fine as a fancy lady's talcum powder. The dust just swirled up and around us, getting into our hair, our eyes, our throats, and down into our necks, where it rubbed against our sweaty collars.

The thunder just rolled all day and by the time we got to White House, which was about fifteen miles from where the fighting was, you could see low clouds of smoke far away. It got dark and we bedded down in a field, but all night long you could see flashes of light far away, like heat lightning in a summer sky.

We were nervous and quiet, wondering what tomorrow would bring.

Come dawn we were told that we would be held in reserve to guard supplies and the bridge at White House, which crossed a small river. Now down deep that made me feel two ways at once. Part of me was really disappointed because I thought we would get up into the battle. There were all sorts of rumors flying around and some mule skinners told us that the army had cracked clean through the Rebel lines, were into Richmond and the war was just about plum over. Now, that made us feel like we were missing all the fun. But the other part of me was almost kind of glad we weren't going forward. The closer we got to the real fighting, the more I started to think it wasn't going to be anything like we imagined. The sight of that dead soldier in the graveyard sure didn't look glorious to me at all.

The rolling of the thunder continued through the day, and late in the afternoon we saw the first wounded coming back, loaded down on wagons, and you could hear them crying and moaning. With them came rumors that the fight had gone all to hell and was a bad defeat.

It continued like that day after day, just a river of wounded coming back, and gradually we started to find out that near on to ten thousand soldiers were killed or wounded in a big charge that had lasted for not more than a half hour.

An ambulance driver, who stopped when we offered him some coffee, told us that just before the big charge the soldiers already knew they were going to die and that the generals were making a big mistake. He said that the men took pieces of paper, wrote their names on them and then pinned the papers to their backs so people could figure out who they were later.

He said that after the charge the field was carpeted with blue bodies from one end to the other and on their backs the pieces of paper just fluttered. He said, sadly, that writing their names didn't matter none, since they all got shoveled into unmarked graves because there was no time to sort them out.

He cursed horribly against General Grant and General Meade, who was under him. He said Grant was a drunken bastard who was slaughtering the army and that we would be next. He said the problem with the army was that the soldiers were the best fighters that were ever born, just as good as any Reb, but that our generals were a pack of lunkheads and politicians who kept making idiotlike mistakes. We filled his canteen up with coffee; he thanked us and then got in his wagon to head back to where the fighting was.

We stayed there for near on to three weeks and didn't get any closer to the fighting. For the first ten or twelve days that we were there we could hear the thundering of the guns just about every day, especially when the wind was from the west, and then suddenly we woke up one morning and it was still and quiet. After the days of thunder it was strange to hear the silence.

It stayed that way all through the day and on into the next, and even the supply wagons moving up and back stopped. Word finally came up that darned near the entire Army of the Potomac had picked up and moved on south, crossing over the James River and on to the city of Petersburg, which was about twenty miles south of the Rebel capital of Richmond. It seemed that Grant got tired of knocking on the front door of Richmond and had decided to try and cut it off from the south.

That's the first time I heard that town spoken of . . . Petersburg. It wouldn't be the last.

It came on to June the twenty-first, and on that day I saw my first fight.

Chapter 7

★ ★ ★

It was early into the afternoon and another scorching-hot day. We were standing guard duty at the bridge, as we'd been doing for the last three weeks, and I figured by that point that we'd be stuck forever doing nothing but standing around staring at a rickety bridge and big piles of boxes that were filled with food, clothes and ammunition.

I was down near Colonel Russell's tent, sitting under a tree and trying to sleep a bit in the noonday heat. When I wasn't beating on my drum during drills, parades and on the march, I was supposed to stay nearby Captain McHenry and be his messenger and orderly. It was fine work; there wasn't much to do except run back and forth occasionally to the colonel and carry a message. Also, it was good for the food. Officers ate a lot better than the ordinary soldiers. Captain McHenry was convinced that I still wasn't all that much better from my measles and a bit of the two steps that I'd picked up. So he'd always give me some of his dinner and told me I had to eat it all to stay healthy, an order I was more than glad to follow.

So there I was, sort of half snoozing when off in the distance I heard what sounded like popcorn popping. It was just a rattling sound for a couple of seconds and then silence. I didn't think anything of it but then I noticed that around the camp it got real quiet. I opened my eyes and saw the officers standing, looking off to the west, shading their eyes from the sun and staring.

There was another rattling sound, a bit longer than the first, and then a deep, cracking boom.

Colonel Russell came out of his tent, stood there looking and then turned to his officers.

"Get the troops formed, gentlemen. It looks like trouble." With that everybody started to scatter. Captain McHenry came running up to me, grabbed me by the shoulder and shouted for me to follow him and get my drum.

We ran down the row of tents and the men who'd been sitting around their fires, cooking their food, stood up, looking around.

The rattling started again, this time a long, steady rolling.

I got to my tent and, without bothering to put on my heavy jacket uniform, I just reached in, grabbed my drum, slung it over my shoulder and started to beat the roll for assembly.

Men came running from every direction, snatched up their muskets, pulled on their cartridge boxes over their shoulders and formed into lines on the company street. The colonel came riding down the line shouting for the men to form up into column and follow him.

We fell into double time, our company at the head of the column, and ran through a field of corn that was near on to thigh high, the heavy stalks twisting up in our feet and getting trampled under them. From the far side of the field, about a quarter mile away, I could see puffs of smoke and tiny blue figures riding out of the edge of a forest of pine trees, moving fast.

It was hard to see much, just puffs of smoke and Union cavalry troopers riding towards us. One of them suddenly spun around like he'd been hit in the side by an ax handle and tumbled off his horse. It was then that I heard a strange sort of buzzing sound, like angry bees zipping through the air. It was a funny feeling; I knew right away that what I was hearing were bullets, but at the same time I really didn't believe it, like we were just playing at being soldiers and the other side had decided to cheat and put real bullets in their guns.

"Form line of battle, battalion front, and load muskets!" the colonel shouted.

Captain McHenry picked up the command and shouted it out as well. I immediately stopped where I was and just started to beat on my drum to pass the signal along. Just like we were parts of a machine, the long column of men began to shake itself out into a battle line to face whoever was in the woods. In less than a minute our line was formed up. Ramrods were pulled out, and all up and down the line men were tearing open cartridges with their teeth, pushing powder and ball into the muzzles of their guns, and then ramming the loads down.

"A Company, deploy as skirmishers!"

Now, this meant that the men of my company were to move fifty yards or so ahead of the main line, all spread out. That way if there was some sort of trap waiting in the woods, A Company would feel it out first rather than have the whole regiment go stumbling straight into it. It also meant that if there was a trap in the woods, A Company would just get swallowed up, sacrificing itself while the rest of the regiment survived. I guess it's what they called good military logic, but it sure wasn't much of a comfort when you're the one getting sent in first.

We ran out from the battle line and started across the field, the men spreading out, half a dozen feet between each of us. The last of the Yankee cavalrymen, who'd run from the woods, came past us and a sergeant, with blood leaking out of his boot and his face knotted up in pain, rode up to Captain McHenry and reined in.

"Reb cavalry, must be a company or two. They just came ripping down the road and caught us by surprise."

"Get to the rear, Sergeant. Our surgeon's setting up—get that foot taken care of."

"Thank you, sir." I could see that the sergeant was mighty glad we were going in instead of him.

We started across the field, moving pretty fast, and from the woods we could see puffs of smoke and overhead the zip, zip of the bullets kept cracking by. Just to my right a cornstalk suddenly leaped into the air and I thought it was strange that it would jump like that, not even quite realizing that a bullet had torn it loose. We got down to about two hundred yards from the woods and the captain shouted for the men to hold their ground and start shooting at the smoke puffs. Well, with that we opened up, the first shots fired by our regiment. To my left I could see Jim standing there, just grinning with happiness, and I started to feel it as well. We were shooting back at the secess! We were finally in the war.

The colonel came riding up and started talking to the captain as calmly as if they were out for a friendly little jaunt in the fields. The colonel figured that it was just some cavalry on a raid and there was no sense in rushing the men in and getting them chewed up in a charge for no good reason. He said we'd hold the front and let the unit of cavalry that was helping to guard the bridge move to flank them, and the captain agreed.

Our regiment moved up and Company A formed back up into the line. The colonel called for a volley, and every soldier just raised his musket up at the same time and pointed it towards the woods. Hundreds of muskets all fired at once, the field echoed with the thunder, and we couldn't help but cheer. Everyone reloaded and we volleyed again. Off to our right we heard bugle calls and saw our cavalry moving out across the next field and spreading into the woods.

The colonel called for us to cease fire. As the smoke from our guns curled and drifted away, we saw that the firing from the other side had stopped. The colonel told Captain McHenry to run our company forward again and we started out across that field. Now, suddenly, my heart started into pounding. What if them secess was just lying low, waiting until we were right on top of them and then pop up? But the captain didn't seem concerned and said that the Rebs had hightailed it out, what with our own cavalry coming in on their flank.

He was right. We got into the edge of the woods and the first thing that struck me was the smell of rotten eggs, which was from the gunsmoke, and of fresh-cut pine trees. All the trees at the edge of the woods were splintered from our firing, and fresh pitch was just oozing out. The captain told the men to look up and see how most of us were firing way too high—a lot of the trees had been hit ten and fifteen feet off the ground. We didn't see any Rebel dead and I was a bit disappointed in that; I figured there'd be piles of them. All we saw were a couple of trails of blood on the ground, a dead horse, and then off curled up behind a tree was a Yankee soldier. He was all rolled up in a ball, the ground around him torn up where he must have been thrashing around, the pine needles under him sticky with blood. He was dead.

The captain told Corporal Barnes to get several of the men to make a stretcher out of a blanket and some branches and bring the man back. We continued on into the woods, moving cautious-like. Off in the distance we could hear some shooting, but it was getting further away. As we cleared the woods into the next field we saw some horsemen moving on up the road, a good half mile away or more, a tiny red flag fluttering above them. That was my first look at Rebel soldiers.

So that was our first fight. Two of the men in our regiment were wounded, neither one really seriously, and they actually were strutting around, showing off their wounds, and everyone was looking at them like they were heroes or something.

I'd have to say that we felt like we'd fought some really

important battle, but in truth it was nothing more than a little mischief to make the day exciting, unless you were that Yankee we found curled up under the tree; for him, that was the most important battle of his now finished life.

Later that day we saw high-towering columns of dust raising up from the northwest, and then into our camp came regiment after regiment of Yankee cavalry. They were part of General Sheridan's raiders, who'd been riding back and forth behind Rebel lines, just tearing things apart. The month before they darned near took Richmond by surprise and in a fight just outside the city had killed Jeb Stuart, the famous Rebel general.

They were a mighty fine sight; their horses were tired, but most all of them looked of fine stock. For a while I even found myself hoping that I'd see Cassius and Brutus, or some of the other horses that were taken away from the farm down in Kentucky. It made me realize just how far away I'd come because of this war. Three years before I never imagined that I'd wind up with an army in Virginia fighting against the secess to help free my people from slavery.

The following morning we broke camp and started out again, joined up by half a dozen other infantry regiments. We marched along with Sheridan's cavalry, heading south to join back up with the main army, which was now fighting a whole bunch of pitch battles around Petersburg.

The fine weather broke, and come early in the afternoon a powerful thunderstorm came up out of the west. Now, when it got to thundering and lightning I was used to coming in from the fields and sitting in the barn or cabins till it passed. But there was no place for us to go, and, besides, we were in the army and had to keep on moving along.

It was almost as dark as night. We stopped for a moment to pull out our rubber ponchos and put them on, and then started back into marching again. The rain soon came down in blinding sheets, and the lightning cracked and roared overhead. It was terrifying but had a strange kind of beauty to it. When the lightning flashed, the muskets swaying on the backs of the men shined with a deep blue light. I thought of my pa, who used to make lightning rods, and could just imagine him sitting up there in heaven, looking down on us like we were a pack of fools, each of us marching through a lightning storm with a big steel pipe in our hands pointed straight up at the sky. Everyone was really nervous about this, especially after we passed a dead cavalryman and his horse who were knocked over and killed by the storm. But we weren't allowed to stop and the storm finally blew on.

The rain had killed the dust but now it was all churned up into a real gumbo soup of mud, which splattered all over us. It was a hard day's march. I slung my drum up over my shoulder, lowered my head and just kept pushing along, putting one foot in front of the other. My shoes kept making a sucking noise with each step and I had to curl my toes up to keep my feet from popping out. Pretty soon each shoe was weighed down with a couple of pounds of Virginia mud, which, I tell you, is the worst mud in the world. When we took a break I just gave up, pulled my shoes and socks off, and tied them on to my belt. Walking barefoot made it a bit better; the only problem was that a division of cavalry was on the road ahead of us. One second you'd be marching along in the cool mud and then the next you'd hit something a bit warm, which kind of made you wrinkle up your nose a bit and want to shake your feet off.

The sounds of a regiment on the march gets kind of haunting and in my dreams I still hear it at times. First off there's the steady rhythm of the marching, thousands of feet just tramping along. Next you add in the sound of our tin coffee cups that we hooked on to our tarred canvas haversacks, which we carried our food in. The tin cups would bang against our canteens, and with each step that you took there'd be a little tinny rattle of cup against canteen. Next was the creaking of leather: your shoes, if you were wearing them; belts and cartridge boxes; slings of muskets or my drum sling. Then add in the steady patter of talk, men breathing hard, snatches of songs, bursts of laughter, the clop-clopping of horses as officers rode along the line and the whispering of the wind through the trees. All of it added together was sort of like a music of men going to war, a powerful sound, but also kind of soothing and almost dream-like. I sometimes think the roads down in Virginia must be haunted now: all the hundreds of thousands who died there, walking those roads late at night, a ghostly army drifting by, the song of their passing just whispering on the wind.

We camped that night by a slow-moving stream that softly swirled by, and the woods were filled with the sounds of whippoorwills and the calls of sentries. Come dawn, we started up again. The woods were cloaked in a heavy, damp fog that drifted through the trees. We started heading into a swamp, the Chickahominy, which had seen a lot of fighting two years before in what was called the Seven Days Battles. It was a creepy place. There were a lot of places where trees had been cut down to form breastworks, which were now overgrown with creepers and brush. You could see signs of the fighting all around us, trees that had been slashed up by gunfire, bits of uniform moldering by the side of the road, empty ammunition boxes, busted wagons, rotting hunks of canvas, and sections of woods that had been burnt over. The few houses in the area were abandoned and all in ruins, their empty, broken windows looking like skeleton eyes.

We passed a couple of places where men had been buried, one place that was terrible to look at 'cause the graves had been dug really shallow. It looked like wild pigs or dogs had been rooting in the graves. Bones were sticking up out of the ground, and from one grave a skeleton hand was sticking out, a rotting blue uniform still hanging from its arm. The hand was pointing at us and the men all started saying it was the hand of death. We got really quiet at the sight of it.

From up ahead there started to come the steady sound of muskets popping in the woods, and the sound kept growing as we continued down the road. We passed a place where there'd been a brief fight, and three dead cavalrymen were lying by the side of the road with blankets over them, and beside them were a couple of dead Rebs. The Rebs were a sorry-looking lot. One of them had shoes on but there were big holes in the bottoms of them and his pants was so raggy and torn that even a slave would think twice before putting them on. So this was the secess, I thought.

He couldn't have been much older than me. His blond beard was thin and scraggly, his cheeks hollow from not eating too well. As I walked past him I kind of felt sorry for him. He looked so sad and lonely there, his face all streaked with blood and mud.

Some messengers started riding past us, their horses all lathered, and one of them pulled up in front of the colonel and said that he had a message from General Sheridan saying that we were to move quick up the road, that a fight was building up at the bridge just ahead.

We started into double time down the road, the mists swirling around us, and it was an eerie sight. The column ahead would dip down into a hollow that was heavy with fog and disappear, and on the far side you'd seen men coming back up out of the mist. Everything was in colors of gray and white. We'd head down into the damp hollow and it'd get really cool and you could hardly see the man in front of you, and then we'd come back up again.

The sound of fighting was spreading out through the woods and we came up to a bend in the road and there, straight ahead, was a rickety old wooden bridge, made out of logs, that went over the Chickahominy River. From the other side of the creek you could see puffs of smoke swirling out, and overhead in the branches you could hear bullets humming by, smacking into the trees.

I was right up at the front of the column. A cavalry officer was talking real excited to the colonel, saying that the cavalry division had crossed the river and now some Rebs had come in through the woods and were trying to cut the bridge off. We were to get across and then spread out into the woods and hold the road.

The colonel told the flag bearers to uncase the flags and they were pulled out of their canvas covers and unrolled. The colonel got off his horse, stepped out in front of us and said that when we hit the bridge to move fast.

We started out at a quick walk and then straight ahead was the bridge and the colonel started to run. We all took off after him. Along the sides of the creek we could see dismounted cavalrymen firing away. Some of them had the fancy new Spencer repeating guns that could fire off seven shots before having to reload and they were just blazing away. The creek was foaming up where bullets were splashing and it was all making an infernal racket, bullets zipping by, water spraying up with loud splashes, and everywhere men screaming and hollering.

We hit the bridge at a run and started across. It was tough going since the bridge was made of split logs and it was hard to keep your footing. I heard a grunt, looked over my shoulder and saw one of our men double up and drop right over the side of the bridge into the creek. We kept on running and got across, the far side of the bridge being held by some more cavalrymen who were pointing for us to turn into the woods to our left. The colonel told us to keep moving down the road. It was hard to see much, what with the fog and the smoke drifting around.

We could hear men yelling in the woods and I saw some fellows coming out carrying an officer and there was a big ugly red hole in his uniform, blood just pouring out of his stomach and dripping on the ground under him. He was talking half crazy, screaming some woman's name and then telling the men to put him down and go back into the fight and then screaming for the woman again.

The colonel hollered for us to halt and to load. The road echoed with the clatter of ramrods scraping in muskets, and then next he told us to fix bayonets. The shiny steel blades flashed out and were fastened on to the ends of the guns.

We turned and went into the woods.

I stayed close behind Captain McHenry. The fog and smoke muffled the sound so that it was hard to tell where the shooting was coming from. Officers started shouting for us not to shoot unless we were really sure it was a Reb in front of us. I saw some men moving up ahead through the mist and thought I'd die of fright until I realized they were on our side. They looked back at us and I could see they were a bit startled by a solid wall of black soldiers suddenly appearing as if out of nowhere.

"Hey, colored soldiers," one of them shouted.

"I don't give a good damn what color they is, as long as they get these damned Rebs off of us," another yelled, and I could see them grinning at us as we came up.

"Be careful, they're just on the other side of the next gully," one of them said, "thick as fleas on a dog in August."

We pressed on in and sure enough, about fifty yards ahead the ground dipped down a bit, the pine woods thinning out into stinkweed and swamp grass, and then all hell broke loose: a solid wall of smoke and fire flashing out.

Well, it's kind of hard to remember all that happened next. I thought I'd seen a real fight the other day, but that was just a little tea party for old church ladies in comparison. A tree I was

WE LOOK LIKE MEN OF WAR   111

standing next to seemed to explode, spraying me with bark and bits of sap. Overhead a branch as thick as my wrist just got cut clean off and fell down on top of me and gave me quite a start. I lost the beat on my drum for a moment as I scrambled out from under it. All down our line we just opened up and started blazing away. After those first shots you couldn't see anything worth a damn. I'll have to say I didn't see a single Reb, just flashes of fire and smoke that swirled around and choked you and made your eyes water.

I heard a grunt of pain and saw William Day in B Company just go flipping right over backwards. He was hit smack between the eyes. Another fella staggered out of the line, cursing a blue streak and holding his arm. Captain McHenry, with Sergeant Felton beside him, kept walking up and down behind our company, telling the men to aim low, to get behind the trees for cover, to fire carefully. The woods thundered with musket fire and you could hear the steady zip of bullets coming back.

After several minutes of this we could all sense that they were giving way. We pushed forward up out of that gully and a cheer started to build up in our line. It was a deep, bone-chilling yell, almost like we'd turned into mad animals on the hunt. I felt it as well and started into yelling and walking alongside the captain, just beating on my drum.

We cleared up through the gully and came into where the Rebs must have been standing. The ground was littered with torn cartridge paper and I saw half a dozen crumpled-up heaps of what looked like broken dolls lying on the ground. A couple of them were sore wounded and one of them looked up at us, wide-eyed.

"Damn," he snarled, "I done got shot by a damn nigger."

Sergeant Felton stopped for a moment, uncorked his canteen and knelt down and offered it to the Reb, who was shot in the leg.

The Reb took the canteen and gulped some water down. The sergeant took the canteen back and then smiled.

"Son, you got shot by a damned Yankee soldier," he said in his quiet voice. We pushed on and that Reb just kept looking at us, wide-eyed.

We must have advanced a couple of hundred yards further into the woods, which were turning into a thick tangle of swampy ground. Occasional shots would echo out and men in our line would stop for a second, draw a bead on what they thought was a Reb and fire back. I heard a couple of the soldiers shout and jump aside and first thought that maybe a Reb had popped straight out of the ground. Then everyone started into laughing. The scared soldiers had kicked up a rattlesnake, which was just buzzing away angrily until someone shot it.

An officer came riding up through the woods, ducking low to avoid getting knocked down by branches. He saluted the colonel, told him we'd done a grand job, but to hold our line and not go further in.

So we stopped and Company B was thrown forward another fifty yards to act as skirmishers. Everyone was all excited, telling each other all at the same time how brave they'd been, how many Rebels they'd shot and what they'd done. Why, if we'd shot half the Rebs that they were claiming, there wouldn't have been any Rebel army left.

We stayed there an hour or so and then word came for us to pull back to the road and continue on. It was a strange feeling, leaving that place. We'd fought for the ground, a couple of the men in the regiment had died for it and a dozen more had been wounded. It was a fight that stands as next to nothing when compared to the big battles, but it was important to us and now we were leaving the ground we'd won. Somehow it didn't seem right.

We headed back through the woods and found a couple of our men who'd been wounded, as well as a few Rebs, who couldn't get out by themselves. Jim helped pick up one of them and we also picked up our two dead and carried them out to the road.

It was a sad and sorry sight when we got out there. One of the dead men had a brother who didn't know he'd been killed until he seen him just lying there on the ground, his friends standing around. His brother let out a terrible cry and threw himself on the ground, just holding his brother, rocking back and forth and weeping. An ambulance came up to take the wounded and dead away, and they had to hold the brother back when the body was put inside. Colonel Russell went up to him and put his arm around his shoulder and spoke quietly to him. It was a heartbreaking sight as the ambulance rolled away, the brother just standing there, tears streaming down his face, the colonel with an arm around him, and so help me, I could see tears in the colonel's eyes as well.

So we continued on down the road and the rest of the day was like the beginning. We'd hear cracks of shots off in the distance, and then we'd pass a place where there'd been a short fight, a couple of dead and wounded by the side of the road. Messengers kept riding up and down the line all day, and once a whole battery of horse artillery came galloping past.

We came through a little village of several shacks, all of them ablaze, but no one in sight except half a dozen Reb prisoners and a couple of our cavalrymen standing guard. We took a break in the clearing next to the burning village to rest for a couple of minutes.

Sampson White, who was in our company, suddenly stood up and walked over towards the prisoners with a huge grin on his face.

"Why, hello there, Massa!" he shouted and walked up to a Reb officer who looked none too pleased with being a prisoner for starts and now being recognized by a former slave.

"Why, Massa, don't you recognize me?"

The Reb officer finally nodded.

"Hello, Sampson," he said quietly.

Sampson got really quiet then and walked around him. It was obvious that the Reb was getting nervous, especially when a lot of us got up to go over and watch.

Sampson just stopped in front of the Reb captain and looked at him coldly, not saying a word for a long minute. I knew what he was thinking; I could well imagine what I might be tempted to do if it was Ben Washburn standing in front of me. I could see the Reb captain was getting a bit shaky and half expected to get torn apart.

"Well, old Mr. Daniels," Sampson said quietly, "I'd have to say that it looks like the bottom rail's on top now."

Sampson turned and walked away. The dignity he showed in treating Daniels with such contempt, while never laying a hand on him, caused us to cheer.

One of the cavalrymen guarding the Rebs strolled over to join us for a few minutes and seemed mighty pleased with Sampson, laughing at what was said. He told us that they'd been riding all over Virginia like this for the last two months, just smashing up Rebel positions, tangling with Reb cavalry and militia near every day and driving them crazy.

The orders were passed for us to move on, and we continued down the road, Sampson laughing and never looking back, as if by seeing his old master one more time he'd finally left something behind.

We were sent out twice more into the woods and lost a couple more men and another eight or so were wounded. Now, each of those little skirmishes weren't all that much, but it started me into figuring that if we fought a fight like that every day for a month, there wouldn't be all that many of us left. Somehow I had figured that this war would be one big fine battle where we all got to see each other, have at it for the day, and one side would run and the other could strut around and say they'd won. But so far it was skirmishes for forgotten village crossroads or snarling at each other over who would own a bridge for an hour or two, or who could cross a field or stand in a piece of woods for a while. Each time a couple more got killed, and no one even bothered to put a name on the fight. It didn't seem like it was really changing the war, and yet men were dying real regular-like.

As it started getting on to the end of the day, we came up over a low rise of ground and there before us was a big, broad river near to half a mile across. It was the James River and we were told that on the other side was land already held by our side. Far off to our right we could hear a distant thunder and Lieutenant Grant said that was the fighting going on around Petersburg.

The army, he said, had tried to take the town and lost a lot of men, including a lot of black soldiers who'd been in a couple of the charges. The Rebs were well dug in and we were besieging the place. Both sides were digging trenches and forts like groundhogs gone crazy. All we needed to do, he said, was break through the Rebel line and take Petersburg. If we took Petersburg we'd cut off Richmond from the railroads heading south and that would mean that the Rebs would have to surrender their capital city and get out or be starved to death.

So that's where we're heading, I realized. We went down to the river and crossed over a pontoon bridge, which was made out of a road laid over big boats that were anchored to the bottom. There was even a drawbridge in the middle so steamboats and ironclads could go further up the river.

The land south of the river looked a lot better than the nasty tangle of swamps and narrow roads we'd fought through. It almost looked peaceful. None of us knew that we were crossing over the river into the land of death.

Chapter 8

★   ★   ★

We camped on the far side of the river and the following morning started out again, moving up closer to where the fighting was. After several hours of marching on a road that was all churned into dust, we came into a place called Prince George's Courthouse, which was four or five miles away from where the siege lines were around Petersburg.

We were entering into the rear area of the Army of the Potomac and it was like there was an entire city on the move around us, which I guess in a way it was. Long afterwards, when I took to studying up on the army and that battle, I learned that there were over a hundred thousand men with the Union army, and that's even after we lost over sixty thousand in the last month and a half of fighting. That's the main reason why General Meade, who was the officer under General Grant, agreed to have colored regiments: they'd simply been losing soldiers faster than they could replace them.

Our regiment was down to around five hundred men at this point, what with disease and our first battle losses, so if you did a little figuring it came out that we were equal to the losses of about three hours of fighting on a typical day. The army was bleeding rivers of blood. I guess so was the secess army, and when you added it all up there were a lot of hospitals and graveyards just plum overflowing.

Now, to keep this army going there were a lot of supplies and such needed. We saw a bit of this when guarding the bridge and supplies up at White House, but now we were only four or five miles to the rear and we saw a whole lot more. Wagon trains of supplies, which just stretched for miles, came rolling through this little village, and another whole line of wagons was moving back up to the James River to pick up more that were being unloaded from dozens of steamboats. There were wagons stuffed with ammunition, food, clothes, blankets, medicine, saddles, horseshoes, hay, oats, shoes, news-papers from Washington and New York, hats, tents and even whiskey, which had a really big guard around that wagon and all of them looked mighty pleased with their job.

We stayed there for a couple of more days while General Sheridan's cavalry continued on by. I heard that the general himself came up to Colonel Russell and said we were fine sol-diers and that we'd done well in the fight in the swamp. The colonel made sure word of that was passed around and every-one was pleased, because Sheridan was known to be a hard-fighting man. Now, we started to worry a bit that we would be stuck behind the lines again and just stand around all day guarding supplies, watching the wagons roll back and forth and listening to the battle which boomed away off in the distance. I kept thinking of what Mr. Speed had said about how we'd either sit out the war in some forgotten place or get thrown in and slaughtered, and he seemed to be right on at least half of that. I wished he'd stayed right on that first half.

And then I woke up one morning with Captain McHenry telling me to get out of my tent and start beating on my drum for assembly. It wasn't even dawn yet but I roused the men out, with them all cussing at me like I was the cause of their losing some sleep and I was doing it just to be mean to them. We lined up in the early light of dawn and the captain said that a high and mighty general, General Ambrose Burnside himself, was coming to look us over, and word was that we were joining his army corps.

Now, that got us all excited, some of the men cussing and others acting happy, and a regular argument broke out at once over this General Burnside. Some of the men said Burnside was known as a hard-luck man. He'd been in command of 9th Army Corps since back in 1862. At the Battle of Antietam he'd made a really poor show when ordered to get his men across a creek. He wasted half the day just charging straight at a stone bridge and getting a lot of men shot because the bridge was covered by Rebs with cannons. The sad thing was that if he had simply ordered the men to jump straight into the creek, which was only a hundred feet across, they could have just waded across in no time and not even got their backsides wet.

Well, such a brilliant type of fighting just naturally won him a promotion to be the commanding general of the Army of the Potomac. At the one and only big battle he'd run, which was called the Battle of Fredericksburg, he sent his entire army charging straight up a hill against where the Rebs were all dug in. It was sort of like his battle for the bridge, except with a lot more men. It was a slaughter and twelve thousand men were shot for nothing.

So he was demoted again to just running his 9th Corps. Now, some of the men kept saying what a lunkhead he was, but others said that he was a right fine fellow, that he did some really good fighting down in North Carolina, and that he was one of the generals who liked and wanted colored troops. I guess we wanted to be liked so much that we were willing to take anyone who'd give us a chance to fight.

We got the captain to tell us what he thought, and he said

that Burnside was forming up a full division of colored troops. He said that eight other regiments of colored soldiers would be in the division as well, and with Burnside we'd soon get straight into the thick of the fight. Then he yelled at us to get ourselves ready to turn out and to make sure we looked like soldiers.

Everybody ran back to their tents and set to brushing the mud out of their uniforms and to polishing up the brass on their belt buckles and cartridge boxes.

About an hour later we heard shouts of commands for the regiments to form up. Jim came over and gave me a quick look-over. I tried to brush the red mud off the seat of his pants and then we ran over to where the line was forming. As a drummer I was sent all the way down to the middle of the line to stand with the other drummers and musicians behind the flags and then we just stood and waited, and waited, and waited.

I sort of think that there must be a rule that the higher up you are in the army, the longer you have to make other soldiers wait. When they know a group of privates are waiting, I half believe they go off and hide someplace, peek out at us and keep looking at their watches.

"Why, they've been waiting a half hour now under that hot sun," someone would say.

"I'm a general and they's got to wait a whole hour before I show up," someone would say back, and they'd just sit there in the shade, look at their watches, sip on a little whiskey and, finally, when the hour was up, they'd come out to see us.

We must have stood there for near on to an hour and then finally from around a bend in the road we saw a whole knot of officers come riding towards us. I tell you that when a general of an army corps comes to visit, he's got a whole caboodle of really self-important officers riding along with him. Why, there were captains who were decked out in uniforms that looked like they'd cost a year's pay, then there were majors and colonels that looked like they'd just spent the entire day riding around in parades and made sure they ate enough to feed three privates. Finally came the general himself.

He was a jolly sort of fellow, wearing a plain old ordinary officer's coat with no special ribbons or medals on it. He had the funniest-looking hat on, with a broad brim and a rounded crown that must have been a foot high. His sideburns were as bushy as a raccoon's tail and I heard that's how they got their name . . . *Burnside* just turned around backwards-like.

Colonel Russell rode up to him, saluted, and they chatted for a couple of minutes, the general smiling and nodding and then finally reaching out friendly-like and patting the colonel on the arm. We were all standing at attention and they rode over to us and started down the line. He stopped right where I was, standing right behind our regiment's flag. He saluted it and the United States flag alongside.

"Heard you boys seen some mischief when marching with Sheridan," he said, looking down at Sergeant Felton.

"Yes, sir, and we licked them," the sergeant said back and the general grinned.

"That's the spirit, son. Well, you're going to see some more fighting real soon and I'm counting on you boys of the Twenty-eighth to show the Rebs what colored soldiers, fighting for freedom, can do."

All of us just broke into grins at how friendly he was. He gave us a cheerful wave and then moved on down the line. Now, as soon as he got friendly, all the other officers got friendly too, I guess because they figured it was allowed. They smiled at us, asked us what we thought of the army and the food and were we ready to get into a real fight. I guess if the general didn't like us, those same officers would have made ugly faces at us and cussed us out.

They rode on down the line and stopped. Commands were shouted down the line and we drummers commenced to beating on our drums, the fifers to fifing and the buglers to blowing. The regiment formed up into a column and paraded down the field, all of us singing "The Battle Cry of Freedom":

"And we'll fill the vacant ranks,
"With a million freedmen more,
"Shouting the Battle Cry of Freedom!"

The general saluted as we marched past, and I can tell you, everyone was bursting with pride.

That evening the colonel called us all together and told us that we were now officially part of Thomas's Brigade, of Ferrero's Division, of Burnside's 9th Corps, of the Army of the Potomac. What this meant was that we were part of a brigade which was made up of five regiments, ours being the fifth while the other brigade had four regiments. There were two of these brigades to our division, which totaled a little over four thousand men, and there were four divisions in Burnside's corps, making a total of around twelve thousand. The other three divisions were white soldiers who'd seen a lot of fighting, and they didn't number as many as us in a division.

The regimental quartermaster showed up and went from company to company, passing out the cloth badge of our corps, which we were to sew onto the tops of our caps. The badge was a small shield with an anchor on it and the whole thing was green. The green color meant we were part of the Fourth Division and the anchor and shield showed we were 9th Corps. We were really proud of those badges since they meant we were officially part of the Army of the Potomac. With a corps badge on his hat, you could tell right off where a soldier was from. If he had a red cross on his hat, the red meant he was with the First Division, and the cross was the symbol for the old 5th Corps. A white cross would have meant the Second Division and a blue cross the Third Division.

The following morning we packed up our gear and moved again, this time only a couple of miles closer up to the front. We came around a bend in the road and there ahead of us were long lines of army tents set up in open fields, and we saw just hundreds of black soldiers coming down the road to greet us.

Now, our brother regiments were the 19th, 23rd, 29th, and 31st. The 29th United States Colored Troops were a lot like us, being recruited from Illinois, while the 31st were from New York. The 23rd and the 19th were both recruited in the South, one in Maryland and one in Virginia, and they were near all to runaway slaves.

They cheered us as we came in and I tell you, it was a proud moment for all of us. Soldiers were asking where we were from and there was a big commotion when a corporal in the 29th came bursting through the line and just grabbed hold of one of the men in Company B and started to hug him, both of them just crying with joy. The corporal was the son of the soldier in our regiment. He'd run away before the war from down in Tennessee, and his father had come north looking for him after our army had taken the farm where they lived. And now here out in a field in Virginia, they'd finally found each other.

Well, word of that shot through the lines and everybody just started into cheering. Our march kind of broke down at that point, the men just mingling, talking, laughing with each other, all of us united by our freed chains of slavery, and now united as an army coming to finish off a world that had held us in those chains.

Several soldiers let out a whoop of delight when they saw Sergeant White and rushed up to hug him. Parson White being Parson White, he fell into a quick sermon on how we were all brothers united together and everybody listened to him, even the white officers standing by respectfully, taking off their hats when the parson asked us all to pray together for victory and freedom.

That done, the officers shepherded us back into line and we continued up the road, falling out where a section of a field had been set aside for us. After we pitched our tents, laid out our company streets and cooked a bit of dinner, the officers gave us the afternoon off to visit with the other regiments. It being Sunday, Parson White organized a prayer service, and hundreds of soldiers from our regiment and the others, hearing how he was a powerfully good preacher, came over to listen. He picked right up on what he'd talked about down on the road, how we were all brothers united together and that we would prove to the world, if need be by our blood, our right to be equal citizens in the United States of America.

I think it was some of the finest preaching I ever heard. He took us through the history of our bondage, the two hundred years of suffering under the lash, and we wept with him when he told us of our grandfathers and their grandfathers before them. Then he came up to us, how we had risen to the call, had escaped from slavery, dressed in rags, with nothing to call our own except our souls, and now we were coming back as liberators for those of our brothers and sisters still in chains.

And then he told us of what was to come. How there were many who still were not willing to see us as equal, how there would be hard times of proving, of standing up, until there came a day, maybe not even in our lifetimes, when our children and the children of white folks would see each other as equals in the sight of the Lord, and the sword of war would be buried forever and replaced by love for each other.

Well, I tell you, I'm not ashamed to admit that I was choked up a bit by the end of it. And when I think of what he said all these years later, I still feel a hard lump in my throat. At that moment I stood with my hat off, surrounded by the men of which were now my army, and I believed that all things might be possible. I guess I still do.

The prayer meeting broke up and Jim and I set off to wander around the camps. It was strange to visit with the men from Virginia. The way they talked sounded strange. Some of them were runaways from North Carolina and South Carolina and they were even harder to understand, and talked with what we figured must be a lot of African words. But their stories were the same as ours and we laughed together, imagining what our old masters would think if they could have seen us now.

The brigade we joined had seen some hard fighting up at a place called Bermuda Hundred and had been in on the first couple of days' fighting in front of Petersburg. They said that the front was a terrible place. Both armies had dug down deep, the trenches sometimes not a hundred yards apart. Sharp stakes were driven into the ground in thick tangles, and deep holes were dug all in front of the trenches to slow down any attackers. You ran a mighty big gamble if you tried to stand up and stretch, because Reb bushwhackers were just waiting and they could shoot the eye out of a squirrel at a hundred yards. They said that sooner or later we'd see it for ourselves.

We had supper with some of the men from Illinois, one of them being right from Perryville. He'd even known my pa, and it made me feel really proud when he said that my pa was a good and honest man.

Night finally came down and we went back to our camp. It was a beautiful evening, the stars out in the heavens overhead, campfires springing up, the sound of laughter and singing carrying on the evening breeze. The air was rich with the smell of wood smoke and frying bacon and it felt awfully good to be alive. Things finally settled down and come ten o'clock, we heard a bugle call. It was different from what I was used to hearing and Captain McHenry said it was a new bugle call named "Taps." It sounded really soft and peaceful, almost making you want to go to sleep. I'd yet to hear it played at soldiers' funerals so I didn't feel a sadness yet. Even now, hearing it makes me think of that night, of being happy, proud and kind of sleepy after an exciting day. It played over us real soft-like, and we went to sleep.

The next couple of weeks didn't bring anything of real excitement. We were being held in reserve a couple of miles back behind the line. There'd be days where it was really still up at the battle front, and then there'd be a whole big ruckus of artillery fire. At night we could see the flashes of light and the lazy tracing of mortar shells rising up into the sky. Sometimes they'd burst and would look just like a Fourth of July rocket going off and we'd lie out in the field and watch the show.

I guess I was one of the first in the ranks to figure out something was up. I was up near the colonel's tent, after running a message up to him from Captain McHenry, when a messenger came riding in, saw me and asked where the colonel was.

I led him over to the colonel. The colonel read the message and called for his horse. He rode off, and I didn't think anything of it. He came back a couple of hours later and he seemed kind of strange, sort of excited; but at the same time, as he rode through the camp he looked at the men real serious-like. Under his arm was a rolled-up piece of paper, which I figured was a map, and he went into his tent. A couple of minutes later he came out, saw me and told me to run and go fetch the captains of our six companies.

I went running through the camp, found each of them and then tagged along behind Captain McHenry when he went up to where the colonel was waiting, sitting under a tree. The colonel told them to sit down, then called for a couple of corporals to post a guard and told them that no one was to come near the officers while they talked. So I got shooed away, but I saw the colonel roll out that map and start to point, the other officers looking at it, nodding, pulling on their beards, a few of them lighting up cigars, which they always seemed to do when they had some powerful thinking to do.

I went back to the camp and saw Sergeant Felton and told him what I'd seen.

"Now, drummer boys ain't suppose to be spreading wild rumors and you know better than that," he said.

"But what do you think it means, Sergeant?"

The sergeant smiled in his fatherly way and told me to go run along or he'd find me some nasty chore to do like covering over a latrine pit.

I knew then for sure that something was up. That evening Jim Barnes came in to where we were sitting and said that he'd been talking with Billy Baker, who was the cook for the headquarters officers. He said that Billy told him that the officers were all excited and he heard one of them say that if the plan worked we would win the war all by ourselves. Then Jabez Mitchell, who'd gone up to the doc to get a boil lanced where he sat, said that he heard the doc saying to an orderly that he was sending him back to the supply center at City Point to try and scrounge up some more bandages and chloroform because we would need more supplies really soon.

By the time we were to go to sleep the whole camp was just buzzing away and the sergeants went around all in a lather telling us to shut up and stop gossiping. But the sergeants seemed worked up and excited too, and that just made us even more certain that a big battle was brewing.

★   ★   ★

The following morning we were roused out along with the other regiments in our brigade, and together we marched out to a big open field about a mile from our camp. There were long strips of cloth tied to stakes set in the field so that it looked like somebody's laundry had blown away. Captain McHenry told us that we were going to practice some maneuvers.

We were led up to where there was a long strip of cloth and told to form up into a big column, one company behind another, five regiments deep. So there we stood, fifty men across and forty lines back, and we covered near on to an acre of ground. Right next to us was the other brigade in our division, formed up the same way we were.

General Ferrero, who was the commander of our division, got out in front of us and gave us a little speech. He said that we'd been given a really important assignment. He couldn't tell us what it was yet, but he said that if we did our jobs right, we might very well be responsible for winning the war in one big final attack. He told us we would practice our attack over and over again till we got it down so that we could walk through it in our sleep.

He finished talking and rode off to one side. Colonel Thomas, who was the commander of our brigade, now got out in front of our big column and said that for starters we would walk through our attack plan. He pointed his sword forward and told us to advance at the walk.

We started across the field, and it was sort of like a parade. I was up in the front line, marching beside our flag, and Colonel Russell was out front with us. He had his sword out and marched backwards, watching us, shouting commands for us to keep our lines close together. We went about a hundred yards across the field, which sloped upwards, and reached another line of stakes. Smack in the middle of the hill there was a big circle drawn out, marked with more stakes driven into the ground and closed off with long strips of canvas. Our column stopped for a moment. The officers went over to that big circle, shaking their heads, talking and pointing, and then came back.

The column alongside of us, which was the other brigade of four regiments, now turned to the left and moved around the circle and we continued on and moved to the right.

We got just past the circle on the ground and then stopped again while the officers looked at maps, argued and talked a bit more. Then Colonel Thomas went back to the 29th, which was last in the line, and had them swing out of the column and change their formation from a block column into a line. What that meant was that we would continue to move straight west in a big block, while the 29th turned to the north and changed themselves into a line. They then started marching away from us heading north. I looked over to where the other brigade was and they were doing the exact same thing, except they were pulling one regiment out and having them march southward.

Captain McHenry was watching this. Sergeant Felton asked him what it meant and the captain said that we were practicing to charge the Rebel lines. Once we broke through, some of the men were to move off to cover our flank and push the Rebels further back from the hole we'd made in the line.

The sergeant pointed to the big circle which was drawn out between us and the other brigade and asked what that was for. The captain smiled and said he couldn't tell us but we'd know soon enough.

They marched us forward again and the 31st Regiment was finally pulled off from the back of the column and made to swing in alongside the 29th, which was still marking off to the west.

Finally we were several hundred yards past the big circle and there was another line of stakes and strips of cloth and we moved through that line. At that point they had us all turn to the north and form up into lines while the other brigade, which was a hundred yards off to our left, was turned and faced to the south.

Now, this had taken us the better part of a couple of hours to do, and once it was done they turned us around, marched us all the way back to where we'd started and then had us walk through it all again. Towards the middle of the afternoon we saw General Burnside himself come riding over to watch us and gave him a big cheer. He grinned real happy-like, waved to us, and we could see he was pleased, nodding with approval as we marched through our drill again.

We did it again and again for the rest of the day. That night we were all stirred up talking about what this meant. It was obvious that we were going to be in a big battle and that we would attack a secess trench that had two lines, one about three hundred yards behind the other. But nobody could figure out what the big circle in the middle of the first line was all about.

Some of the men from the Maryland regiment came over to visit with Sergeant White and they told us they'd seen charges made against Rebel trenches, had been in one themselves, and said it was a slaughter.

For the next week we kept doing the same drill day after day. They started us moving a little bit faster each day, until finally we could do it on the run from start to finish with our eyes closed. I even took to dreaming about it. Next they sent us out at night, and though we got a little confused at first, we quickly mastered doing it in the dark as well.

After near on to ten days of this they had us go up to the practice field and we spent the whole day digging trenches where the Rebel line was traced out. Then we cut down trees and made tangle barriers out of branches and sharpened stakes in front of what was supposed to be the Rebel line.

Next we made small wooden bridges which were about a

dozen feet long and looked like stretchers for a giant that were carried by eight men. The next day we marched out to the practice field again. The men in the front ranks carried axes and the next line had men carrying the wooden bridges. The order was given to charge and we ran forward across the first stretch of field and got up to where the stakes and branches were all piled up. Now, that stopped us cold and the men behind us started to bunch up, the officers shouting, cussing and trying to keep them in line. The fellows in the front rank leaped forward with their axes and chopped down the stakes and branches we'd built the day before. Within a minute we'd cut a hole through and moved forward. The men carrying the wooden bridges now threw them across the top of the trench and we then ran right over the trench and pushed on.

Now, that started me to thinking and made my blood feel a bit cold. You see, I started to realize that charging a Rebel trench would not simply be running straight at their trenches and leaping over them. We'd have to stop thirty feet in front of the trench and just stand there out in the open until the stakes and branches were cleared. A lot of men were going to get killed in that first minute.

When we were done our officers marched us down the hill and a regiment was left to rebuild the damage. An hour later we did it again. Except this time there were a whole bunch of officers standing by the stakes. We charged up to them, and the front rank of men armed with axes leaped forward to start cutting down the tangle barrier. The officers then started grabbing hold of men who were chopping and shouted for them to lie down and drop their axes. Sergeants now shouted for men in the next line back to leap forward, pick up the axes and keep chopping. Pretty soon there must have been sixty or seventy men lying on the ground. Now, a lot of them were laughing and groaning, making a big show that they were shot, which got the officers mad. Since Jim was so big he was one of the men given an ax, and it gave me a really bad feeling when an officer suddenly grabbed him and told him to drop the ax and lie down.

When we got the holes cut we continued forward, and now the officers started grabbing hold of men carrying the bridges and telling them to fall down and for other fellows to pick the bridges up. Now, with this everything just started to fall apart. The men in the back couldn't see what was going on up front and kept pushing forward. Everyone started getting all bunched up, shoving and pushing, and in all the confusion the officers were just cussing at the top of their lungs. Half the wooden bridges were trampled under and some of the men were knocked into the trenches, one of them screaming and cussing that his leg was broken.

Colonel Thomas finally pulled out his revolver and fired a shot in the air and everyone got quiet. He was damned near purple with rage and chewed us out really bad, saying that we had to get it right or we'd all get killed for real.

They marched us back down the hill again, fixed up the branches and stakes, and we did it all over again. It took a couple more days of practicing and finally it all started to fit together. We got to the point where we'd go straight up that hill on the run, come to a stop, and even if the officers knocked down a hundred men we'd cut our way through, lay the wooden bridges over the top of the trenches and then charge straight on up to the next line and spread out and start moving north, the other brigade doing the exact same thing and spreading out to move south. After that they had us go out to the field to practice it just after sundown. It finally got that we could even do it all in the dark.

General Burnside showed up again and watched us practice. When we finished he seemed as pleased as a dog given a knucklebone. He got off his horse, walked around and shook the hands of the regiment commanders. Now, they in turn were all pleased and came up to us, and pretty soon everyone was slapping each other on the back and shaking hands. Colonel Russell told us that the general had said he'd never seen any troops, white or black, look so good, and he was certain that when the time came we would win the war in one glorious charge.

Chapter 9

★   ★   ★

A couple of days later Sergeant Felton came up to my tent before dawn and told me to fall out and to make sure my uniform looked smart. I was still rubbing the sleep from my eyes as I followed him up to the colonel's tent. The colonel took a look at me, said I looked all right, and I noticed that the six company commanders were there, along with a couple of staff officers. Captain McHenry came up and told me we were going on a little walk and that I should come along as an orderly and messenger. He smiled and said that we might see a little action and asked if I was afraid.

I just grinned with delight and he patted me on the shoulder.

The officers started off, heading up to the front, and were just chattering away. I knew better than to start butting in with questions but I kept hearing them talking about "the mine," as if it was really important to the plans, and they kept wondering if it was done yet.

Now, what a mine had to do with us I couldn't figure out, but I knew better than to ask.

Day was just about on us, and up ahead the sound of artillery fire was really sharp and clear. We came over a low rise of ground and straight ahead, maybe three quarters of a mile away, I saw a long line of red dirt and a couple of United States flags flying over the trenches. Beyond that first line was a forest of stakes and an open stretch of ground maybe a hundred yards or so wide and then there was another line of trenches with stakes in front of them. Smack in the middle of the next hill was a big fort made out of earth, rising up from the trenches, and it looked awfully ugly and threatening. Over the fort I could just make out a tiny red square of cloth floating over it. It was the Rebel lines.

We passed some breastworks. Inside them were six of the shiny bronze Napoleon cannons, their crews lounging around and watching the fireworks. We continued across the field and passed another set of breastworks, and inside them were four big ugly-looking black guns. They were mortars and looked almost like big, thick church bells pointing straight up. Their crews were hard at work, loading them up. The crews stepped away from the guns and a major stood up with his hand raised high.

"Fire!"

The gunners yanked on the lanyards and the four guns went off with a deep, throaty thump. It was a strange sight. You could actually see the mortar shells pop out and rise up into the air. In the light of early dawn the burning fuses traced a trail of fire. The shells rose up higher and higher, then seemed to hang in midair, and then started back down towards the Rebel lines. I saw four flashes of light and seconds later came a distant rumble. Then from the Rebel lines we saw two trails of fire rise up. I watched them really close and the officers around me got quiet and watched as well. The shells continued to climb upward and seemed to stop almost straight overhead.

"To the left, fifty yards," Colonel Russell said, but to me it looked like they were coming straight on down. You could hear the whistling of them. I wanted to duck but I was too ashamed to let the officers see I was afraid. The shells tumbled down and hit the ground off to our left, just like the colonel said they would, and they exploded with a loud clap. The colonel looked over at me, saw I was still standing and smiled at me.

We continued on across the field, and overhead I could hear the occasional hum of a bullet whistling past. Just when I started to think we were getting a bit close to things I saw the beginning of a trench, which dropped down into the ground, and we got into it. The trench was more like a tunnel covered over with boards and logs that had dirt piled on top. It was called "the covered way." We hiked for another quarter mile or so inside the trench, when the colonel stopped for a moment. We had reached a stretch of low ground between the hill where the batteries were and the next hill up, where the Rebel lines were on top.

The colonel stuck his head up out of a hole in the side of the covered way and pointed.

"This is where we'll deploy out before the assault," he said, looking back at the officers.

"We might be spotted from the Rebel lines," Captain McHenry said.

"We'll move up shortly after midnight. It's set to go off at three-thirty, so it'll still be dark. The main thing is to keep the men quiet. Tin cups are to be left behind, canteens are to be full and secured, and all talking is forbidden.

"I want all of you to look this ground over really carefully. It's the only time you'll see it in daylight. Our jump off line will be marked with white strips of cloth, so we should be able to find it even in the dark. Now, once the show starts, we head straight up the slope, over our own line of entrenchments, and then on up the hill just like we've been practicing. Our line of entanglements and stakes will be cleared by pioneer troops during the night, and footbridges will be laid over the top of our own trenches.

"Every artillery piece on the line will open up as well. At

the start they'll be firing straight overhead towards where the mine lets off but they'll lift their fire once we get over our own entrenchments. In the dark it might be kind of scary to have those batteries behind us cutting loose, so make sure your men are told about it beforehand."

The officers all nodded and a couple of them asked questions about things like defilade, fields of fire and other such military talk.

We continued up the trench towards the front. We had to step aside for a moment while some stretcher bearers came through, and they were carrying an old, gray-bearded soldier who was shot right in the temple. He was stone dead and wasn't a pretty sight.

The colonel told us to keep our heads down. The covered way finally came up to the end and led straight into the main battle line entrenchments. It was crowded with tired and dirty-looking soldiers who were sitting inside small little caves dug into the ground. Everything was covered with a thick coating of red dust, and I tell you, it stank something awful, sort of a cross between a garbage pit and an outhouse that was set to overflowing.

The trench was real deep, seven or eight feet in places, and there were little platforms set along the side where a man could stand and peek over the top. General Burnside, Colonel Thomas and General Ferrero were there along with a whole bunch of other officers. It seemed like near every officer in our division was there and the trench was just packed with uniforms with shiny bars and such on their shoulders. I felt a bit nervous, being a lowly private and drummer boy in that crowd. It was kind of funny 'cause Colonel Russell suddenly turned around and saw me. He grinned a bit and winked at me as if to say that there was nothing to worry about and then he kept on going. We fell in behind the crowd of officers, walked for a hundred yards or so, and came to where there was a square hole cut into the side of the trench facing the Rebel lines.

"Well, this is it, gentlemen," General Ferrero said. He pointed at it real proud-like, as if that hole was somehow his doing. I'll have to say I didn't like him for some reason, and I found that my gut feeling about him later was proven to be right. He was the lowest kind of officer.

"Colonel Pleasants, why don't you explain it," and the general pointed to a short colonel who was really thin and had a pointy sort of beard.

The colonel stepped forward from the side of the hole in the ground and nodded a greeting to the officers.

"I'm Colonel Pleasants of the Forty-sixth Pennsylvania. It was my regiment that dug the mine."

Now, that still had me confused; why were they digging mines? I wondered. Surely they weren't looking for gold or something with a war on, but the other officers looked at him real respectful-like so I figured it was something important.

"The mine goes down thirty feet underground and then runs for nearly five hundred feet straight up to the Rebel lines," the colonel began. "It stops directly under the Reb fort up there. We've dug two side galleries, each about forty feet long, running directly under the Rebel fort from one end to the other.

"Starting tonight, we'll put twelve thousand pounds of gunpowder into those galleries."

"I thought it was supposed to be twenty thousand pounds," Colonel Thomas said.

"General Meade's refused our request. He stated that his engineers said it'd be a waste of powder to use twenty thousand pounds." I could hear in the colonel's voice that he wasn't at all happy.

He looked over at General Burnside, who gave his usual

friendly smile and just shrugged his shoulders as if to say it wasn't his fault.

Twelve thousand pounds of gunpowder under the Rebel fort? It suddenly hit me that this wasn't a mine to look for gold, it was a tunnel under the Rebel fort and they were going to blow the whole damn thing up! That's why they had that big circle drawn in the field where we were maneuvering and practicing. They were going to blow up the fort and then we'd charge past the hole that was left!

"What can we expect from the explosion?" Colonel Ross, who was in charge of the 31st, asked.

"Well, as near as I can figure it's going to be the biggest explosion in history, twelve thousand pounds of gunpowder all lighting off at once. I estimate that it will blow a giant crater a couple of hundred feet across and maybe thirty feet deep into the ground. That Rebel fort will just simply disappear and there'll be nothing but a smoking hole in the ground. Them Rebs will get blown halfway to heaven."

"God help those poor bastards up there," Colonel Russell whispered, and a lot of the men nodded in agreement.

"The most important thing to remember," General Ferrero said, "is to keep our men moving once the mine is blown and the attack begins. Now, with luck it'll scare the hell out of the Rebs in the trenches to either side of the fort and they just might pick up and run for all they're worth."

"Hell, I sure would" came a voice from the back of the group and everyone laughed.

"We've got to move in fast and every second will count. We might have five minutes, maybe twenty or thirty before they get their wits back and try to seal off the hole. In that time we've got to cut through."

"You've got to make sure that none of the men actually go into the crater," Colonel Pleasants said. "That hole will be a death trap if your men simply run up, take the crater and go no further. The Rebs will reorganize, pin you down and then wipe you out."

"Our men have been training for weeks," Colonel Thomas said. "They know what to do."

"I know that," Colonel Pleasants replied. "It's just that our army's taken a hell of a battering the last three months. A lot of boys have learned that a hole in the ground is a mighty safe place when the bullets start to fly and they just might see that crater as a safe place to be."

"That's why we're using fresh troops," Colonel Russell said.

"Don't worry about it, Colonel," General Burnside said. "The division of colored troops is trained for a breakthrough attack; they'll get the job done right."

"I'm sorry, sir," Colonel Pleasants replied. "It's just that I've seen our army throw away too many chances for victory by some last-minute screwup. I've got my heart set on seeing this thing work and finishing up this damn war so we can all go home."

General Burnside gave Colonel Pleasants a friendly smile but I could see that he was none too pleased by what the colonel had just said.

The two stared at each other for a moment and then General Burnside turned away to look back at the rest of the officers.

"First off, we cut our way through the entrenchments to either side of the crater," Burnside said. "Thomas, your brigade to the right and, Sigfried, yours to the left, like we've been practicing. You each peel off one regiment to turn and push the Rebs further back from the break and the rest of you charge straight on ahead. I want a breakthrough five hundred yards across within twenty minutes after the mine explodes.

"Our first goal, gentlemen, is Cemetery Hill, which is four hundred yards behind the Rebel fort. There might be some artillery there, we're not sure. Starting tomorrow General Grant will launch some attacks up near Richmond to try and draw the Rebel reserves off. We figure they might just pull their guns out and move them.

"Once we get to Cemetery Hill we'll be on the Jerusalem Plank Road. Gentlemen, if we cut that road it's finished for the Rebs. That is the main road to the Confederate lines south of Petersburg. Take that hill and we've made the breakthrough we've been dreaming of for months.

"But that's only the start, gentlemen." I could see that he was getting excited. "If we take that hill behind the Rebel fort, I think we just might finish up this war by the end of the day."

General Burnside looked over at Colonel Thomas, our brigade commander.

"Colonel, I hope you realize how important this is," the general said quietly. "Get your brigade on that road and then all you have to do is turn north, just like you've practiced. The city of Petersburg will be eight hundred yards away. You'll be behind the Rebel lines at this point. I want you to charge that city. I'll be pouring the other three divisions of my corps in right behind you. But you'll be the one leading the way. Fifth Army Corps, to our right, will also pour in all its reserves once we've made a clean breakthrough. That means there'll be over twenty thousand men coming in behind you, Colonel Thomas."

Colonel Thomas, his face calm, nodded.

"There's a lot at stake here," the general said. "If this plan works we'll cut off most of the Reb army south of town and capture their main supply base of Petersburg before they're even half awake.

"I tell you without exaggeration that it'll mean the end of the war." His eyes were shining with excitement. "With Petersburg captured and the Rebel army cut off to the south, it means that the Rebel capital of Richmond will be defenseless.

We'll take Richmond within a couple of days. Down south Sherman's knocking on Atlanta's front door and between that and our taking the Rebel capital, it'll all be over. Make this attack successfully and the war will be over within a month. Colonel Thomas, it'll be your men who will lead the way to final victory and everlasting glory."

The colonel broke into a grin.

"If anyone can do it, my men can, General."

General Burnside nodded.

"I don't think I need to tell you, Colonel, what else rides on this," and he turned and looked at the other officers.

"A lot of people are still saying that black troops can't fight. You men became officers of colored regiments because you believed differently. I've watched you drill for this attack and I'm convinced that if anyone can do it, your men can. Now, I want you to think about this. The attack we're going to launch here might go down in the history books as the battle that won the war. Think of what it will mean if it's colored troops that do the winning. I think, gentlemen, it'll change forever how the two races see each other. I want you to tell your men that when you finally explain to them what will happen two days from now. I want them to know what it is that they will be fighting for out here. No matter what other folks might say, I believe that this war started over the crime of slavery. I think it would be a powerful statement if it was former slaves who finished this war, saved the Union and ended slavery forever."

You know, after thirty years I still remember that talk as if I heard it just this morning. I stood there in awe, feeling a tingling all over. I thought of my pa, hoping that he was looking down from heaven, seeing what his drummer-boy son was about to do. I thought of my ma and how proud she would be. I thought of all the Ben Washburns in the world and how never again would they be able to look me in the eye with that sick look of contempt like I was lower than a dog. I honestly felt at that moment that if I were fated to die in this battle, it would be worth it.

The meeting ended and we headed back up the covered way. Colonel Russell looked over at me and put his hand on my shoulder.

"So what do you think, Sam?"

"By God, Colonel," I replied. "It's gonna be black troops who win this war."

The colonel looked kind of sad and thoughtful.

"Let's hope so, Sam, let's hope so, but I tell you, there's a far piece to go from talking about winning and then actually doing it, and sometimes it's our own generals that make it harder."

I was shocked to hear him say that and I guess he was a bit surprised too, 'cause he dropped his hand from my shoulder and continued on.

It turns out, of course, that he was right.

That evening Colonel Russell held an assembly for the regiment. He had the men break ranks and gather round in a big circle and explained what was going to happen, tracing it out with a piece of charcoal on the side of a canvas dining fly. He told us, the same way General Burnside did, about what it might mean if it were black soldiers who captured a Rebel city that had stood off the whole Union Army of the Potomac for nearly two months.

With that we were dismissed for the evening.

We gathered around our campfires and this evening there was no joking or laughing and storytelling. Everyone was really quiet and serious. We knew now what it was that we'd been preparing for, not only in the last couple of weeks of drill, but back all the way since we joined the army and long before. We knew now that for all of us, that first stirring of long ago, that first dream of freedom and an end to slavery, had led us to this moment. We were about to face our fiery trial, and like President Lincoln had said in one of his speeches, it would light us down in honor or dishonor throughout history.

It's a hard thing to ask men to die and it's a hard thing to know that, come another day, you might be doing the dying. But I can tell you that in all our hearts, at that moment we were willing to do just that. I get kind of frustrated in the telling of this part of the tale. I think about what I just said, and somehow the words I'm trying to say just can't ever tell it all. We looked at each other and smiled kind of sad-like, knowing that more than one of us would not be here in another day. We'd never again see a sunrise, hear the robins singing in springtime, or watch the leaves turn colors and fall, or hear that wonderful sound of a baby crying its first breath of life. But it would be worth it if we died knowing that our people who were born after us would make that first cry breathing the air of freedom.

It started real soft-like, a lone voice rising up, singing a couple of words, and then drifted back down, just like in church when the spirit moves somebody to sing. The voice, a deep, rich bass, sang the words again, and then from another part of camp a high, clear tenor picked the words up and sang them again.

"We looks like men a marchin' on. . . ."

The first note was real high and then dropped down low.

The words drifted across the camp, a few more voices picking it up.

And it floated back and forth for a couple of minutes, drifting from campfire to campfire, more and more voices adding in.

Then another voice came in and added the second line.

"We looks like men of war. . . ."

It seemed to shoot like an electric spark through the camp. Within seconds hundreds of voices picked it up, took hold of it, raising themselves up high, the words echoing across the plains.

> "We looks like men a marchin' on,
> "We looks like men of war."

I ran to my tent, got my drum and beat out the rhythm of it, adding a militarylike roll at the end of the two-line song.

Men started to clap their hands to it, and the fifers added their song. Everyone was on their feet, clapping, singing, near all of us with tears in our eyes.

I saw Colonel Russell come out of his tent, other officers joining him. As if they were in church, they took their hats off and walked through the camp, their voices joined in with ours. The song drifted on the wind and echoed through the night.

> "We looks like men a marchin' on,
> "We looks like men of war."

We were told the following morning that we would run the practice one more time and then take the afternoon off for sleep. We got all lined up and everybody was really serious, all of us knowing that the next time we did this it would be for real. Just then we heard a commotion and saw a bunch of generals riding up. The word just shot through the ranks that it was General Meade himself. Now, General Grant was the commander of all the armies, and even though he traveled with us it was General Meade who directly commanded the Army of the Potomac and was General Burnside's boss.

They rode by and stopped for a minute, looking us over. We just stood there and I could see that General Burnside was mighty upset, shaking his head and pointing at us. But General

Meade looked even madder and he made a gesture that was kind of strange, a wave of the hand as if we were being dismissed somehow. They turned and rode on. I could see Colonel Russell watching them and the colonel looked mighty troubled.

We did the practice one more time and as we cut our way through the stakes I kept looking over at the big circle of ground, thinking how it would look tomorrow, a giant hole where a Rebel fort used to be and all the men inside it dead.

We marched back to our camp and the colonel made sure we got some good food. They'd brought in a couple of head of cattle, slaughtered them, and we all had fresh meat for a change rather than salt pork and we even got fresh loaves of bread to go with it. After our noonday dinner everyone was lined up, sergeants inspected the men, and we marched by companies to a line of supply wagons. Each man was handed eighty rounds of ammunition, forty rounds to go in our cartridge boxes and forty in each man's pockets. Four men in each company were detailed to carry two extra boxes, each with a thousand rounds of ammunition inside, for when we went into the charge.

Then we were given three days of rations, the usual salt pork, hardtack, coffee and sugar, and told not to eat it all at once, since it'd have to last. Then we went back to our camps, rolled up our tents and packed up our gear. Most of the men had long ago thrown away their backpacks and carried their gear in a blanket roll. You'd spread out your poncho, then put your tent half down on top of that, then you'd place your blanket down and on top of all that toss in an extra shirt, some clean socks and whatever else. Then you'd roll it all up, tie off the ends so it looked like a horse collar and sling it over your shoulder. Everybody packed their gear up like that but we were told that we'd leave all that behind and our equipment would be moved up to us later, after the battle was over. Finally, we made sure our canteens were full and our tin cups were all left behind so we wouldn't make any noise.

I didn't like the idea of leaving my Bible and McGuffey Reader behind so I wrapped them up in a piece of cloth and stuck them in my haversack along with my rations.

Everyone settled down, stretching out on the ground, and now all there was to do was to wait. The sergeants told us we should all get some sleep but that's a bit difficult to do when you know that come tomorrow morning, you're going to be in one hell of a battle.

Colonel Russell walked through our company, stopping to talk to each of the men. He came up to me and smiled.

"Well, Sam, you ready to beat the drum for the charge?"

"I'll be right alongside of you, Colonel sir."

"You're a good soldier, Sam. I'm proud of you."

He touched me on the shoulder and then went on. I could hear a bit of a catch in his voice. I knew what he was thinking when he looked at us—how many of us would still be alive come tomorrow?

I settled down beside Jim and we just sort of small-talked. We laughed a bit, a quiet, sad kind of laughing. I guess both of us wanted to tell the other how much we cared for each other but when you're fourteen and eighteen—well, fellows just don't do that.

We started to doze off and then Jim rolled over and nudged me.

"Sam, I want you to do something."

"What is it?"

"If you don't see me after tomorrow, I want you to promise to go back to Indianapolis."

I got a bit upset with his talking.

"Don't be so foolish; of course I'll see you again."

"Now, just listen to me, boy. When this here war's over

with, I want you to go back and finish that schoolin' with Miss Latimer. I want to knows that you made somethin' of yourself. The thought of you gettin' book learnin' will make all this worth somethin' in my mind. You'd be the first of our family ever to read and be educated. Now, you promise me, boy."

I laughed a bit to hide how I was feeling and told him I promised. He smiled, gave me a friendly little punch on the shoulder, then lay back and pulled his cap down over his eyes.

I started to doze off and then I heard some really loud cussing coming from where the officers were. I sat up, looked over and saw Colonel Thomas and all the other colonels of our brigade standing in a circle. They were hopping mad. We all started to sit up and look over and they didn't seem to notice at first that we were hearing them.

Our own Colonel Russell was just furious. He got so mad that he tore his hat off, threw it down and then kicked the fire, knocking over a coffeepot, which sent up a shower of steam.

"He's a damn fool!" Russell shouted. "I tell you Meade's a damn fool! I was with that idiot at Gettysburg and so were the rest of you. He threw away the best chance we ever had to end the war and now he's doing it again. It'll be a slaughter."

Colonel Thomas got really mad as well, especially when he looked over his shoulder and saw all of us watching. He pointed straight at Colonel Russell and I could see he was chewing him out a bit. Colonel Russell lowered his head, nodded and then picked his hat back up.

I could see, though, that Thomas was just as upset and was pacing back and forth, talking and waving his hands. Thomas said something, the officers saluted and then walked off back to their regiments. Colonel Russell came towards us and Captain McHenry stood up as he came closer.

"Sound assembly," the colonel said, and I could see he was still fuming.

The captain motioned for me to get my drum. I stood up,

put it on and sounded assembly. The captain told us to form up but to leave our gear on the ground.

We got into line and the colonel paced back and forth waiting for us. Everything got really still and then he faced us.

"Men, there's been a change in plans," he said and we could see he was trying to act like it was no big thing to worry about.

"We're not leading the charge."

Now, with that a groan went through the ranks and more than one man started to cuss. Sergeants yelled at us to come to attention and we quieted down.

"We're to be held in reserve. The first division of Ninth Corps will lead the charge instead."

This was met with stunned silence on our part. Now, on the one hand you might think we were relieved; we'd just been told that we weren't going to lead the charge and it meant that we'd most likely live to see the end of tomorrow. But that wasn't how we felt at all. We wanted that charge, we wanted it because we needed to prove something, and beyond that we knew that if anyone could win, it was going to be us.

"How come they ain't lettin' us lead the charge?" a soldier shouted out from the ranks, and there was an angry chorus of agreement.

The colonel extended his hands for us to quiet down.

"I'm as disappointed as you are," he said. "But remember, we're soldiers and it's our job to obey orders. Now get some sleep. We're still going to be in reserve and chances are that we'll be in the fight anyhow. I want you men to know I'm proud of all of you and I expect you all to do your duty no matter what it is."

He turned around, walked away, and we were dismissed.

After that it was impossible to settle down and we argued the point back and forth.

"I'll tell you what it is," James Barnes said. "They didn't want niggers leading the charge that won the war."

Sergeant White, who'd been walking around the camp, heard James say that, came over and chewed him out, saying that we were soldiers and that come tomorrow we'd still get a chance to prove ourselves whether we were first in the charge or last.

Long years after that day, I finally came to read how James wasn't that far off the mark, since there was an official court, called by the United States Congress, to investigate what happened in that battle.

It seemed that General Meade from the beginning didn't believe that the idea of blowing up the mine was ever going to work and that's why he cut the powder in half because he thought it'd be a waste. He let General Burnside plan the attack anyhow and then, on the morning before the charge, when we saw him riding with the general, he announced that he didn't want our division to lead the charge even though he knew for weeks that we were practicing for it.

Now, General Burnside got all mad since we were the only troops that knew how to do it right. General Meade said that he still figured that the attack would fail and if it did, there might be a lot of folks who said that the colored division was thrown in first because nobody would care if it was a bunch of colored soldiers that got themselves killed for nothing.

General Burnside was really hot now and said that if the colored division did lead the charge he was certain it'd win. Now, afterwards, some folks who were there said that there was another side to it, that General Meade and some others felt that if the battle was a big victory, they didn't want colored troops leading the charge that won the war. So either way we were out. If we lost they were afraid that people might get upset that we'd been slaughtered, but on the other hand, if we won, folks might get upset that it was colored, rather than white troops, who did the winning.

Damn it, why couldn't they just have looked at us as soldiers who knew our jobs and be done with it?

So, anyhow, General Burnside went all the way to Grant to complain but Grant, who didn't like Burnside, agreed with Meade and that settled it. Now comes an even worse part. Burnside was a funny sort of man. There were times when he could be really smart-thinking, just ready to try new ideas, like black troops, for example. Then there were other times his brain just seemed to get a real case of the slows and he couldn't think worth a damn. This was one of them. Here he had only about twelve hours to go before the attack and his plans were all changed. So he called together his division commanders and asked them what they thought. They all just sort of looked at the ground and hemmed and hawed 'cause, you see, none of them wanted to lead the charge.

Finally the general said, Why don't we draw straws and see who gets to do it? Now, if that don't beat all. So they drew straws and the worst damn division commander in that whole army got the short one—General Ledlie.

He was a no-account fool of the first order. If I met him on the street today I think I'd spit on him and he'd most likely crawl away like the coward that he was. So General Ledlie gets the job of leading the charge. Do you think he immediately went out and got his brigade and regiment commanders together, hunkered over maps and sat up through the night making sure everything was done right?

He didn't do a damned thing. I notice that just in the last couple of minutes now I've said *damn* several times; well, I feel like saying *damn* fifty more times, one right after the other, and a lot of worse words besides. 'Cause this general passed the order on to the brigade commanders under him, said that when the mine blew up they were to charge to the crater and then didn't say anything else!

He didn't tell them the full plan, he didn't tell them to move to Cemetery Hill, he didn't tell them anything other than to charge the crater. He didn't even tell anyone to get footbridges to cross over our own trenches or to clear the sharpened stakes out from in front of our own trenches. Then he immediately went to the rear, a good mile from where the battle was to be fought, found a bottle of whiskey and got himself stone-cold drunk!

It seemed that General Meade started a ball rolling, what with believing the attack was a crazy scheme which was going to fail. Grant caught this feeling, then General Burnside was paralyzed in the brain by it, and soon everyone who was supposed to be running the attack just sat back and started to drink, or didn't do a damned thing.

I thank God that at least we poor bastards who were supposed to do the fighting didn't know any of this at the time, because if we had I think we would have shot the whole lot of them, and come to think of it, maybe shooting a couple of them, especially Ledlie, would have been a good idea.

So we just settled back down and let the time roll slowly by. The sunset was really pretty, with streaks of gold and orange; it got darker and the stars came out. The night sounds, of crickets, whippoorwills and the occasional hoot of an old owl, were peaceful-like. Up at the front it was really still as well, and I dozed off.

I felt Jim's hand on my shoulder waking me up. We stood up and it was chilly. We were told to line up and some torches was lit. Our column formed up and we started out, following some cavalrymen carrying torches who were acting as guides.

We left our campsite behind and obeyed orders that no one was to talk. The column weaved its way through the fields and woods and off to our right we saw another column moving up through the shadows, which we figured was another one of the divisions. Something got mixed up and they came straight down into the road we were on. There was some cussing and yelling and everything got all tangled up for what must have been near to an hour or so before they finally cleared the road ahead of us and we moved on. Just before we came over a rise in the ground the torches were put out. There were officers standing by the side of the road and they kept repeating over and over again, "No talking, move quietly, we're getting near the Rebel lines."

We started down the long, sloping hill and in the dark shadows I could see the outline of one of the artillery batteries we'd passed when I'd come up with the officers two days before.

Suddenly we stopped; there was a whispered argument up front, and I heard Colonel Thomas cussing again. It seemed where we were supposed to be, they'd placed another division instead, but no one had told him this. What was making it even more confusing was that our own division commander, General Ferrero, couldn't be found anywhere to help sort things out, and for that matter the general of the division located where we were supposed to be couldn't be found. Of course, none of us knew that both of them were stinking drunk by this time.

We finally shuffled around to the left a bit. Our formation was all knocked about and men were mingled in with regiments they didn't even belong to. We finally hunkered down and were told to wait.

In spite of the confusion, you could feel the excitement and tension in the air. Even if we weren't leading the charge, we still might get in on the tail end of things. And besides, we were about to see the biggest firecracker explosion in history.

We sat there on the ground and waited and waited. You could feel the tension just building up. In the shadows I saw Colonel Russell, and officers kept coming back and forth and whispering to him.

"It's damn near four o'clock," I heard Russell finally whisper in an angry voice. "It's a half hour late, damn it, it's starting to get light out, and they'll see us."

I looked back to the east and, sure enough, you could see the first faint streaks of light on the horizon, Orion just hanging low there in the sky. It made me think for a minute about the first night that Jim and I ran away and we followed the North Star as our guide to freedom.

The minutes drifted past and I no longer had to squint to see the colonel. It was like a curtain was slowly being pulled back.

"If they don't blow it now, we're going to have to abandon this position. The Reb guns will tear us apart out here," the colonel snapped, looking over at his staff as if they were somehow to blame.

Colonel Thomas came up and looked around, obviously nervous.

"Think something's gone wrong?"

"I don't know what the hell to think."

Thomas looked around again. It was getting brighter out by the second and you could even see the faint outline of the Rebel fort way off on the top of the hill.

"Get somebody up to the mine and find out what the hell is going on," Thomas snapped.

The colonel looked back at our lines.

"Sergeant Felton."

The sergeant came up and saluted.

"Get up to where the mine is, find out what the hell is going on and tell them if they can't blow it within the next ten minutes that we'll have to abandon our position and fall back to cover. Now move it."

The sergeant hesitated.

"Colonel sir, I'm not sure where the mine is."

The colonel looked around and his eyes came to rest on me.

"Sam, you remember the way back up there?"

I stood up.

"Sure do, sir."

"Guide Sergeant Felton there. Now, don't get lost, son. I'm counting on you."

I unhooked my drum and we started off at a run, cutting straight across the open field, keeping low. I started to get scared, figuring that if I could see the Rebel fort outlined up there, maybe they could see us moving across the ground. But I didn't say anything. The sergeant told me to keep low and we crouched along as we ran.

I looked back up at the Rebel lines again, looked down, and then I sort of felt a flash of light as much as seen it. I looked back up again. It looked like the entire top of the hill was just rising straight up into the sky. It was all dark but in the middle you could see a boiling ball of fire shooting up. There was no noise yet, but the ground under my feet started to shake and then the sound hit us, this thundering roar that was so loud I covered my ears and just stood there. The shape of the explosion was still changing, spreading out, and all lit up now by flame. I saw a whole artillery piece, which must have weighed over a ton, just tumbling through the air. I also saw bodies, lots of bodies and, even more horrible, just the parts of men spinning end over end. The whole thing seemed to hang there in the heavens, the flame continuing to race out, clouds of smoke swirling around, and everything just shaking and roaring. And then it all started to tumble down.

From where we were standing, about two hundred yards behind our trenches, it looked like it was almost straight overhead. Hunks of dirt and rock, some of them as big as a small house, came smashing down in the open field between the Rebel lines and ours. Smaller pieces came further out and Sergeant Felton told me to duck. We crouched down, but I still looked up, and a regular hail of rocks and dirt came swirling down. Now off to our right was the whole First Division, lying down on the slope of ground just behind our trenches and in the forward trench line, and pieces of dirt and rock came tumbling in on top of them. The men started to get up, a lot of them running towards the rear, and their lines were getting all jumbled up in the confusion. I could see already that the attack would get off to a bad start.

My regiment had been trained only yesterday morning to expect this—that we were to lie low and cover our heads till things settled down and then get up and charge.

Well, I just stood there awestruck and I have to say I can't blame a lot of those men that started backing up, 'cause it looked like the whole world in front of us was just getting ripped apart and that the gate straight down into hell had been blown open.

A billowing cloud of smoke and dust swirled out and over us and it got so you could barely see. Another sound started in now as well. Thousands and thousands of men started into yelling and cheering, and I guess mingled in from the other side was the screaming of a lot of men who were dying and a lot of others who had just been scared half to death.

The dust and smoke parted for a second and the most amazing thing of all was going on right in front of me. Just out in front of our trenches was a Rebel soldier, at least I figure he was a Reb. He didn't have a stitch of clothing on; he was all cut up and burned. He was just staggering around in circles like someone had poured a gallon of whiskey down his throat. A couple of men crawled out of the forward trench, went up to him and pulled him in to safety.

War's kind of strange; first we blew him up and then right away a couple of fellows risked their lives to save him. I guess the poor fellow could be said to be the first man that ever went flying like a bird. He must have been blown darn near a hundred yards by the explosion and he was still alive. You could see the bits and pieces, though, of a lot of others who weren't so lucky, and it was hard to tell they were even human.

"I guess we got the answer for the colonel," Sergeant Felton said in his really quiet voice. I looked up at him and he was grinning.

"Come on, Sam, all hell's breaking loose; we better get back to our regiment."

Chapter 10

★　　★　　★

Sergeant Felton and I ran back to our lines. Everyone was on their feet just hollering away and grinning with joy. Now that I was away from directly in front of the mine, and the dust and smoke had settled down somewhat, I could see a lot better. Where that secess fort had been there was nothing but a huge hole in the ground with wreckage blown all the way down to our own lines. You could see Rebs just skedaddling like mad, running from the trenches on either side of where the explosion was. I almost felt sorry for those poor bastards. They must have gotten the scare of their lives when that explosion lit off. Captain McHenry said the entire Rebel army would need brand-new clean underwear after that explosion and we all just roared with delight.

All up and down our line the artillery started to fire, the ground trembling beneath our feet, the thunder of the guns soaring to a crescendo of noise that seemed to be struggling to match the explosion of the mine.

We stood there and waited for the assault to go in, and then we found we just kept on waiting. Now, according to the way we'd been trained, the charge was supposed to start right after the explosion and before the smoke and dust had blown away;

that way we'd catch 'em while they were still running. But no charge was going in. We looked down to our right, to the position we were originally supposed to be in, and the soldiers down there were still all milling around. It must have been a good ten minutes or so before the bugles started blowing and the drums rolling. Their formation was all gone and they just sort of started forward, a few men here, a company or two there, and then finally all of them just started out.

They got up to where our lines of trenches were and then it all slowed down again. Some damned fool had forgotten to make sure that there were footbridges for the men to cross over the tops of our own trenches, while the fellows down in the trenches didn't even have ladders so they could climb out. I suddenly realized that right in front of our own line the rows of stakes and tangled branches hadn't been cleared during the night the way they were supposed to be.

I could see the men jumping down into the trench and then crawling back up out the other side. The first ones out just weaved their way through the stakes, which tangled up the ranks even more. Finally a stream of soldiers started across the field, in bunches of two, three, and half a dozen, like an undisciplined crowd walking home from the circus. At this point a good fifteen minutes had passed.

We all had been cheering them to start but now we were getting quiet. You could hear our men groaning, cussing, yelling for them to charge, to move faster, like we were urging on a horse on which we'd bet every last dime we'd ever owned. In a way you could say we were betting our lives that they would do it all right.

The soldiers continued on up the hill but not many of them were running. They stopped to gawk at all the wreckage. Some of them commenced to poking around, picking up things, or standing in knots and looking at some of the dead. We could see a couple of officers running around, pointing with their swords, yelling, and finally the men started forward again. Pretty soon there were hundreds of them heading up towards the Rebel lines. Now, all during this time a shot hadn't been fired from the other side. From our own side all hell was breaking loose; near on to every cannon for miles on either side was shooting. A storm of shells was screaming overhead and just plastering the Rebel lines to either side of where the hole had been blown.

Well, our men finally got to the top of the hill and then we saw the damndest thing of all, which made all of us start to yell and groan. The attacking column simply went up to where the crater was and they started jumping down into it!

We didn't see a single formation of soldiers move to either side the way we'd been trained to do. The ones coming up from behind followed the ones ahead like they were sheep. As fast as they went up into the Rebel lines, they simply jumped into the hole. We started to see some puffs of smoke from over to the right of the crater, and a couple of men out on the open ground between the two lines spun around and went down. That started everyone into moving faster now. The entire division, near on to three thousand strong, ran up the hill following the ones ahead of them and jumped down into the hole.

As I look back on it all now, I guess I really can't blame them. They were good soldiers and had been in a lot of fighting. They'd charged Rebel lines before and got chewed up really bad. After a while you just sort of had an instinct that when the shooting starts, you find a hole and get down into it. Here was the biggest hole in the world right in front of them. And besides, we later found out they hadn't been told any differently. A lot of them said they'd just been told that there'd be a big explosion and they were to run up, take the Rebel line, and that was it. No one ever said anything about spreading out, or pushing on ahead to capture Cemetery Hill and then swing into the town. And as I already said, their commanding general was a mile away to the rear, sitting in a bombproof shelter just drinking away. It turned out that not only was he back there, but so were the division commanders of the other three divisions of our corps, and to top it all off, General Burnside and General Meade were back a mile or so behind the lines as well.

It was a hell of a way to run a war. I'd heard about a lot of good fighting generals, men like Phil Sheridan, who was usually right up in the front of the charge, or like Winfield Scott Hancock, who was shot stopping Pickett's charge at Gettysburg, or that general from Maine named Chamberlain who was shot six times during the war leading his men. Well, by damn, if one of them had been running the whole show that morning, instead of the lunkheads we had, it would have gone a hell of a lot different.

We just stood there and couldn't believe what we were seeing.

After about a half hour there was a steady patter of musket fire coming from up by the crater. We could see where some Rebs were moving back into the long sections of trenches which they had run away from and could have been taken by one lonesome drummer boy like myself.

The firing started getting thicker and heavier. From down off the hill I saw an officer come running and I think he was that Colonel Pleasants who'd thought up the whole thing to start with. We saw him go running on down the hill past us to where the Second Division was waiting in reserve. A couple of minutes later the Second Division started up the slope and we all started into cheering again, figuring that now, at last, it would all be set right.

Some footbridges had been set up over our own trenches, and with our stakes now knocked down the men quickly moved onto the open ground between our lines and the Rebel position. They just went charging straight up that hill and we were waving our caps and yelling.

And they charged straight into that crater and disappeared! Now we started getting really anxious. Colonel Thomas was fit to be tied. He kept pacing back and forth, swearing a blue streak, and sent one messenger after another running back to find General Ferrero, General Burnside or even General Meade to give us the order to go in and straighten things out.

From up where the crater was, a river of blue started to limp back, men holding their arms, their sides or using muskets as crutches. The Rebs started to move closer in and sweep the open field between the lines with fire so that the wounded started getting hit again and the men went down and stayed low.

Messengers on foot, and even a few on horseback, were moving back and forth and you could just smell the confusion. It looked like nobody knew what they were doing and nobody seemed to be in charge.

There was another cheer from our side and we saw the Third Division going in. An occasional Rebel shell or bullet started humming our way but we didn't care. We were on our feet, shouting, straining forward, urging them on. As they got out into the open field between the lines, the Rebs hit them with a volley and it looked like a whole line just simply went down. They pressed on forward and this time, at least, some of them tried to spread out to either side and break the hole open. But now it was costing hundreds where two hours before we could have had that land for free.

Colonel Thomas was in agony and finally he just couldn't stand it anymore.

"By God, I'll get us into this fight one way or the other!" he yelled. He got on his horse and went galloping back towards the rear lines.

Everything was madness. The thunder of our artillery behind us was just deafening and the ground was shaking like it was the beginning of Judgment Day. It was getting hard to see with all the smoke. Wounded who'd managed to get out were coming our way and they were a sorry-looking sight, all covered in blood and staggering along in shock at what had happened to them.

From out of the smoke we saw a colonel come running up; it was that Colonel Pleasants. He must have thought that when he first dreamed up the idea that it was a way to end the war, and now it was starting to come apart.

"Where's General Ferrero?"

Colonel Russell came up to him.

"I'm damned if I know."

"Well, damn it," Pleasants screamed, "what about Colonel Thomas?"

Russell pointed to the rear.

"He's gone back to get orders to attack."

"By God, you've got to come up right now." Pleasants was still screaming. "Your men know what the hell to do. We can still break through but we've got to move now! We can still win this thing."

Colonel Sigfried, who was in charge of our other brigade, came running over and Pleasants told him the same thing.

The three stood there as if frozen. There wasn't any general anywhere to tell them what to do.

"Get ready to move out," Pleasants shouted. "I'll get the orders," and he ran back towards the rear.

A couple of minutes later we saw Colonel Thomas riding back up the slope, lashing his horse.

"Let's go!" he screamed.

He pulled up in front of us and got off his mount.

"Where's Ferrero?" Sigfried shouted.

"Hiding with the rest of them bastards. He said he'd direct us from the rear, but Burnside told me to go in and see if we can save this thing."

Thomas looked back at us while Sigfried ran over to his brigade, which was lined up alongside of us to the left.

Thomas cupped his hands around his mouth.

"Load!"

Men rammed bullets in, ramrods rattling.

"Fix bayonets!"

It looked like a forest of sharpened steel had suddenly flashed to life over us.

"Remember what to do. Remember, the cause of the Union and freedom rest today in your hands! Now, follow me!"

Thomas started off at a quick walk.

Our column moved forward, two thousand men stepping off at once; to our left Sigfried's brigade moved forward as well. We were a solid wall of men over a hundred yards across and a hundred yards deep, our battle flags flying overhead. I picked up the cadence of the march and started beating my drum.

Tha-rump, tha-rump, tha-rump, rump, rump.

We reached our forward trench line and the advance slowed down for a minute as we swarmed over the footbridges across the trench, some of the men having to jump down and then climb back out again. The trench was just packed beneath us with wounded and dying men. A lot of them looked beaten, but at the sight of us they started to cheer, waving their hats, screaming at us to give the Rebs hell, and I was filled with pride. These were my comrades cheering us on.

The cheer started to get picked up by us as well, and then above the roar we heard a voice start to sing.

"We looks like men a marchin' on.
"We looks like men of war!"

The song echoed through our ranks, the tempo of it matched to my drumbeat and the rumbling thunder of our marching.

We got out into the open field and the colonel turned, looked back and held his sword up.

"Charge!"

To our right, up on the hill, a wall of fire erupted from the Rebel lines. The impact of that volley staggered our line. You could hear the bullets screaming through and the horrible *thwunk, thwunk* sound of bullets hitting bodies.

Men just pitched over, knocking other men who hadn't been shot flat on their backs. The song died away into a terrible scream of pain and exploding rage. We broke into a run and I started to just bang on my drum as fast as I could, screaming at the top of my lungs, running up that long, sloping hill.

It looked like it would just stretch on forever and I felt like I was running in mud up to my knees, the type of running you do when you're having a terrible nightmare and no matter how fast you try to run, you feel like you're crawling through molasses.

A hail of bullets screamed over us and I could feel the heavy thumping of the Rebel artillery in my chest. A hot slash of artillery canister slammed into our ranks, catching us on the flank, and a dozen men went down at once. I saw Sampson White go tumbling over, his chest exploding with blood. As I ran past I saw him looking up at me, a scream pouring out of him.

"Charge! Damn it to hell! Charge!" and then he was gone.

We hit the front of the Rebel trenches to the right of where the crater was. Sections of stakes had been torn away by the charge of the Third Division and we poured through, all of us screaming at the top of our lungs. We hit the Rebel trenches and there was fighting going on down in them, our men and theirs just all mixed up together, while further to our right we could see Rebs coming out into the open, formed into a loose line, just pouring shot into us.

"Keep going forward!" Colonel Thomas screamed.

We slammed the wooden footbridges down over the trench and poured over, while behind us the 29th turned to the right like it was supposed to, and started to move towards the Rebs to cover our flank.

But I could already see that it was going wrong. The Rebs were hemming us in too close to either side of the crater. What was supposed to be clear ground, with a scared enemy running from the big explosion, was now an insane battlefield.

I caught a glimpse of the crater to my left and it looked like a madhouse. Thousands of men were packed down inside of it. A lot of them hunkered down, doing nothing; others hung on to the edge and fired.

Up ahead we could see where there was a thin line of our soldiers trying to push forward towards the road. In the crush of men around the crater we slowed down as we tried to push our way through the confusion. I heard later how a lot of our men were getting pushed into the crater and out of the fight. It was impossible to see what was going on with the brigade on the other side of the crater.

But Colonel Thomas and Colonel Russell were still out front, waving their swords, screaming for us to move. We pushed forward, running past the crater, and got up to where the line of Union soldiers was trying to hold on a hundred yards ahead.

I could see flashes of light through the smoke up ahead and the bullets were still screaming in. Every second another man went down. Colonel Russell shouted for us to change from our column into a battle line for the attack, and I started to beat out the signal, the buglers adding their call. The men of the 28th swung out into a line two deep and spread out across a hundred yards or so. Another regiment, from our brigade, came up behind us. All mingled in with us were white soldiers from the other divisions and they seemed mighty glad that we were joining them, cheering us on, swearing at the Rebs, and hollering that now we were going to win.

We started forward and I was still beating out the roll, my hands almost numb from the effort. A spine-chilling roar of rage and battle fury was screaming out all around us and my voice was part of it. I don't think ever in my life, before or since, have I felt such a moment. All my anger at the years of slavery was getting yelled out, at Ben Washburn, my ma being sold, my pa dying, all of it wrapped into one convulsive scream of pain and rage. And at the same time there was a strange sort of hope tied into it all.

The smoke started to part and we could see the Rebs breaking and running. The best that the South had to throw against us, and they were running!

I could hear someone screaming for us to charge and I started forward at the run, still beating my drum. From the corner of my eye I saw Jim, his eyes afire, his mouth open, his hat gone, holding up his musket with bayonet pointed forward.

We ran across that field, jumping over trenches and obstacles, the Rebs pulling back, some of them turning and still firing, men going down around me. A few of the Rebs stopped, refusing to budge, and we charged into them. For a second I saw a Reb coming straight at me, screaming, and then he was knocked over on his back by Jim, who shot him from not more than five feet away, and we went right over him.

And then, just up ahead, I could see it. It was a low crest of ground, a small cemetery, and a road running beyond it. Off to my right I could see the church spires of Petersburg. It was there, so close I felt I could reach out to touch it. The end of the war, the end of slavery and victory for my comrades and me. Victory was just in front of us, not a hundred yards away.

It looked almost like a dream that was just floating out of

reach, so close you could almost touch it . . . and then you reach out and the dream dies.

From out of the smoke along the road I saw batteries of Rebel cannons being unhooked from their caissons and rolled up, and beside them a solid wall of Reb infantry running hard, coming straight at us.

We slowed down, unbelieving. Not twenty minutes earlier and it might still have been ours.

A lone soldier leaped out of our ranks and started to run full out towards the Rebel guns. He slowed, turned and looked back at us, holding his musket high in the air.

"Freedom, boys, freedom. Freedom's just on the other side of this hill!"

We let out a scream and started forward again at the run, a roar of anger in our throats.

The Rebel line stopped; a forest of muskets rose up and then were leveled, pointing straight at us from not much more than thirty yards away. They disappeared behind a wall of fire and smoke. A couple of seconds later the cannons fired, tongues of flames shooting out, each gun letting go with shotgun-like loads of canister.

It was as if our charge had run straight into a stone wall. I tell you that our line just seemed to get picked up and thrown backwards, and you felt as if you had just opened a door into a hurricane.

I got spun around, nearly knocked off my feet, and for a second I thought I'd been hit. I looked down and saw that my drum had been torn in half; the bottom part was blown off. Sergeant Felton went down hard and then came back up, holding his arm; other men were down all around me. I saw Jim suddenly sit down, with a curious sort of look on his face, and I started to scream when I saw the blood oozing out from his shoulder.

We stood there in shock and then those that were still standing raised their muskets and started to fire back. Fire just tore up and down our line and then another blast from the Rebel artillery ripped into us. Lieutenant Grant was standing right in front of me one second and then he was on his back. I still have nightmares where I remember what his face looked like, what little of it that was left to him.

Jim struggled back to his feet and I ran up to him.

"Leave me be, Sam. I'lls be all right in a minute, leave me be."

He looked really pale and I felt like I wanted to cry, but I fought it down; there was too much going on.

The world was thundering around me. There was the deep-throated roar of the cannon, the high, cracking snaps of muskets, men yelling, screaming, cursing, and the angry humming of bullets and the hissing slashes of canister rounds coming in. What was most horrible of all, though, was the clear sound of bullets and canister rounds hitting men. You could actually hear the *thwunk* of the bullets striking flesh and bones.

Our line was staggered but continued to hold, the men on their feet still trying to inch forward, their heads bowed down as if they were walking into a storm. Another blast of artillery slammed into us, and I stood there in horror, seeing men just get torn into pieces, their bodies disintegrating.

From out of the smoke we saw the Rebs moving in on our flank, screaming and yelling, pouring fire into us. It looked like they were going to cut us off in the rear.

"Fall back, fall back!"

I couldn't believe what I was hearing, I couldn't believe that we were actually being beaten. I saw a musket lying on the ground and I guess I just went crazy. I tore what was left of my drum off, ran over and picked the gun up. Screaming, I started towards the Rebs. I felt a hand reach out and grab me.

"You gone crazy, boy, now fall back!" It was Captain

McHenry. I looked up at him in a daze. Blood was streaming from a nasty cut to his cheek and he looked half crazy himself. There was something in his eyes, though, as if he was looking at me like I was a man he was proud of.

"Come on, son, today's not our day. Stand out here and we'll get cut off. Now, help your cousin!"

I turned and looked around me. Our line was breaking apart and another storm of canister ripped into us, picking up men and tearing them apart. Jim was still standing there in shock, and I ran up to him, still holding my musket.

"Come on, we've got to get out of here!"

He nodded, leaned on me a bit, and we started back. The Rebs let out this blood-chilling scream and pushed after us. I saw Colonel Pleasants again for a second; he was by the edge of the crater, trying to convince the men inside to come out and help us, but I guess they could see all too plainly that it was too late.

We fell back, giving ground slowly. We even stopped for a minute to try and form back up. I picked up a cartridge box that was lying on the ground, loaded my musket and then grabbed a handful of percussion caps off the belt of a dead man. I aimed the gun low, like I heard the officers telling us to do, and squeezed. I couldn't see where I was shooting but it made me feel like I was at least doing something, now that I couldn't play my drum anymore.

The Rebs charged in again, this time from our front and our right and we just couldn't hold. The regiment was breaking apart, there was no help coming from the divisions in the crater, and men started to head for the rear.

Jim was getting his head back; he grabbed hold of me, and we started to run. But the only place we could run to was the crater. Off to the side the Rebs were sealing that way off, and men trying to run in that direction were getting slaughtered.

We hit the edge of the crater and slid in, Jim cussing a blue streak over his shoulder.

I looked around and thought I'd fallen into the bottom of hell.

The crater was near on to two hundred feet across and in places must have been thirty feet or more deep. It was packed with thousands of men. Hundreds and hundreds of them were wounded or dead, and the ground was just soaked red with blood. Mixed in was the wreckage of the fort, as well as pieces of cannons just all twisted up like a child's broken toy, pieces of uniform, and pieces of bodies. It smelled like a slaughter-house, which I guess it was.

We were out of the Reb gunfire down in there. I lay back to catch my breath and realized for the first time that it was blazing hot. The sun was high overhead and just beating down on us. Looking at the sun I realized we must have been fighting for a good hour or more. I was awfully thirsty, my throat feeling like it was packed with dried sawdust, and reached for my canteen. It was gone and near as I can figure, when I was pulling off what was left of my drum I yanked the canteen off as well. Jim uncorked his, gave me a long drink, and then he took some as well.

"How's your shoulder?"

"Stings something fierce."

I got him to lie on his good side and opened his jacket up. It was a really nasty hole just under his collarbone, and I felt around to his back and he cussed a bit. At least the bullet had gone clean through. I took his handkerchief and mine, soaked them in water, and packed one in over each hole to try to still the bleeding.

He just lay there panting and cussing softly.

"Here they come!"

I looked up and saw men scrambling back up to the edge

of the crater, pointing their muskets. I still had mine and I crawled back up to the edge of the crater and looked out. The ground up where we'd been was carpeted so thick with blue-jacketed bodies, black and white, that you could have walked from one end of the field to the other and not touched the grass. There must have been a thousand or more dead and wounded out there. A heavy line of Rebs was coming straight at us, screaming and yelling. I started to load up my musket and Jim pulled off his percussion-cap pouch and laid it beside me.

I tried to aim and squeezed off a round, the gun thumping hard against my shoulder, then started loading up again. Again there was this slow sort of feeling, like you just can't do anything fast enough, while the Rebs were just running straight at us, screaming and cursing, their red-and-blue-striped battle flag held high.

I got my gun loaded and brought it up. Not ten yards in front of me I saw this Reb coming at me, his bayonet pointed straight at my face. I aimed my musket at him and fired.

He seemed to leap into the air a bit, the way a rabbit does when you shoot him. He staggered forward, dropping his musket, and then went down on his knees not five feet in front of me.

He just looked at me curious-like, as if I had done something to him that just wasn't fair. I'll see his eyes for the rest of my life. He wasn't much older than me, his red scraggly hair sticking out from under a beat-up old hat. He looked like he wasn't dressed much better than me when I was a slave. His pants was all in tatters, his elbows sticking out from his shirt, and his face was all pinched up from not eating right.

He just seemed to hang there in front of me, his eyes going wide. His hands crept up to his chest and I could see a bright river of blood pouring out of him. I think a sob kind of broke out from me at that moment. I wanted to go up to him and somehow tell him that I didn't mean it—that if he'd just left me alone, I'd have been more than happy to leave him alone as well.

I know I was the last thing he ever saw. His eyes were just staring at me and then they just seemed to go blank, as if his spirit had leaped out of him. He ever so slowly fell over on his side, like an old tree that had finally given up and decided to fall. He twitched once or twice and then was still.

I slid back down into the crater and looked around me. I half expected that every last man down there would be staring at me, ready to point their accusing fingers at me and announce to the world that I had just committed the most horrible sin of all—I had killed a man.

It hit me so damned hard. I didn't think that I had killed a Rebel, or killed a white man, or killed an enemy. I had killed a boy who wasn't much different than me.

But no one seemed to notice. The fighting was still going on and at a couple of places along the edge of the crater, the Rebs were standing and shooting down into the mob trapped below. Men were shooting back up and the Rebs finally broke and pulled back, more than one of them tumbling into the crater to lie with their enemies.

How long this went on, I don't know. I guess two hours, maybe three or four. They charged at least half a dozen more times and I stayed in the fight, though I found that I kept closing my eyes when I shot. It was terribly hard 'cause every time I crawled back up to the edge, that Reb boy was still lying in front of me, his eyes open, and I couldn't bear to look.

It started to get really bad. The sun was directly overhead, just beating down on us. Jim was out of water, as was everyone else, and he was getting a bit crazy, shouting and trying to stand up and then sitting really still and then shouting again. Men were screaming and tearing at their clothes and some of them started to struggle with each other over canteens that were nearly empty. The Reb artillery started to get the range as well and a steady stream of shells came thundering in, bursting over us, showering the bottom of the crater with shrapnel. I suddenly felt somebody tugging on my leg and I looked down to see Sergeant Felton, his arm in a sling.

"Son, we're gonna have to run for it."

"I don't know if Jim can make it."

"Sam, them Rebs are in an ugly mood. We've been hearing that they're not going to take any of us colored soldiers as prisoners. If Jim gets captured, if they don't just kill him out of hand, he'll die in that Andersonville prison for sure. We've got to make a run for it."

"You mean we've lost?"

Up until that moment I had yet to even really think that we weren't going to win. I sort of figured they'd send up more reinforcements; we'd fight our way out and still take Petersburg.

The sergeant looked up at me and actually chuckled a bit and shook his head.

"Son, we ain't ever gonna lose. Just by fighting the way we did, we proved something. But for right here and now, I think we better get out and call it a day.

"Now, let me give you a hand with your cousin."

I looked over at Jim and tugged on his sleeve.

"Come on, Jim, we're goin' home," I said softly.

He seemed to come out of it again and he looked over at me.

"Remember what you promised me, Sam; always remember that."

"Come on, Jim, we're heading back to our lines."

We scrambled down into the crater and started for the slope closest to our lines. Some officers were down in the bottom arguing and they saw us going past.

"Where the hell are you going?" one of them asked.

"Sir, we's gonna make a run for it," Sergeant Felton said.

"Damn it, Sergeant, that's suicide; they're cutting down anyone who moves out there. I'm saying we should surrender while we still can."

"Sir, if you was us, would you want to stay here and wait for the Rebs?" Sergeant Felton asked really softly.

The officer looked at us and shook his head.

"Your men fought gallantly, Sergeant, gallantly. I'm sorry, I'm just so damned sorry." And the officer started to cry and just turned away.

"They're coming in again!"

I saw Rebs just come swarming in, running hard. This time they gained the edge and held on. The ones up front started into firing and as quick as they'd shoot, they'd pass their empty musket back to someone behind them and have a loaded one pushed forward. It was hell on earth. The noise seemed to get caught in that crater and get swirled around and around. Thousands of men were screaming and cursing, the wounded yelling and near everyone off their heads from the heat and thirst. Some of our men were shooting back and Rebs were dropping but then more would just swarm forward. And then worst of all, a cannon was rolled up to the edge of the crater, pointed down and fired. The canister tore through, knocking men over like bowling pins. Men started to hold their hands up, dropping their muskets, shouting that they were giving up. If we were going to get out, it had to be now.

There was a whole bunch of us black troops together and we went scrambling up the side of the crater closest to our lines and moved out into the open. The ground ahead of us was carpeted with bodies, a lot of them still moving, trying to crawl towards safety.

"Start running and don't stop for nothing!" Sergeant Felton screamed and he leaped forward.

We all took off after him. I could hear the bullets zipping overhead and all around me. Hundreds of men were all trying to do the same thing, to get to safety. And somehow it just got me mad again. We were running from a damned bunch of Rebs. It was like I was running away from Ben Washburn, from the men that killed my pa. I was still holding my musket and I turned to aim one last defiant shot.

I half sort of remember Jim turning with me, shouting for me to come on. And then he just seemed to go all loose and saggy like an old doll, the bullet hitting him in the head. I knew he was dead even while he was still standing, as if the Jim in front of me was just made out of clay and dust and he was already gone to someplace else.

I was screaming, I remember that, just standing there and screaming, aiming my gun straight at a group of Rebs that weren't more than twenty yards away, and they were aiming straight back at me. I think I fired my gun; I'm not sure. Maybe it's that I want to remember that I fired one last shot at the men who got Jim.

I don't remember much of anything else, except falling over backwards. I could see the sun and a sky that was filled with smoke. From far away I heard Jim's voice telling me to remember my promise.

And then the world fell away into darkness.

Chapter 11

★   ★   ★

I woke up to pain.

For a moment I thought I was blind and then it came to me that it was getting on to dark. A couple of men were kneeling over me and starting to pick me up. I let out a yell.

"I told you he ain't dead," the one man said, and with that they dropped me.

"Hey, Yank, you got another live nigger over here."

I started to sit up.

"You can go to hell," I groaned, "and I ain't a nigger, you damned Reb."

A couple of other men came up out of the shadows.

"Why, damn him, I'll—"

"Back off, Reb," I heard someone shout. "Rules of the truce are any wounded between the lines we get to take back, so leave this boy alone."

I heard them cursing and they walked away.

I was starting to see more clearly and a man knelt down beside me. He looked at me and smiled.

"How you doin', son?"

"I hurt," I whispered.

"We'll get you taken care of.

WE LOOK LIKE MEN OF WAR

"Hey, let's get a stretcher over here," the man shouted and then he offered me a drink of water.

I tried to reach up to take the canteen but my left arm wouldn't move and when I did try to move it, it felt like somebody had just stabbed me with a red-hot iron. The friendly soldier held the canteen to my lips and put his hand behind my head to help me.

"Seems like you got it in the arm, son, and got grazed on the side of your head too. Another inch to the right and that ball would have gone clean through you and you'd be singing with the angels now. Why, your head's gonna feel like you need a number-ten-size hat come tomorrow, but you'll live."

"What about my arm?"

He patted me gently and told me to lie still and that started me into worrying.

"Why, son, you told them Rebs off just fine. I was proud to hear you sass them back like that, real proud."

I tried to turn my head to look.

"Jim, where's Jim?"

The man turned and looked over his shoulder.

"You know that man there?" he asked really quietly.

"It's Jim. Jimmie, my cousin."

The man sat down, pulled out a handkerchief and started to dab the blood from the side of my face.

"How's Jim?"

"He's dead, son. I'm sorry."

I started to cry, to cry like I hadn't cried since the day I heard my pa had died. The man picked me up like I was a little boy, which I guess I really wasn't all that far from being. He held me in his arms and I just buried my head against his shoulder and cried.

The men with the stretcher came and my friend carried me over and put me down on it really gently.

"Jim," I whispered.

He went over to Jim, reached into his jacket, pulled out his wallet and pocket watch, and gave them to me.

"What's his name?"

"Jim Washburn, Twenty-eighth United States Colored Troops," I said, trying to talk between the sobs.

"I'll see that the Rebs don't take him for burying. I promise you, son. I'll make sure he has the grave of a soldier."

He squeezed my good hand.

"This army's proud of what you men did today," he said. "I'll never forget it as long as I live the way you men charged into those cannons. I'll never forget it. I'll pray to Saint Patrick you get better, son, and for the soul of your cousin as well."

He let go of me and the stretcher bearers took me back down the hill. I never found out who that soldier was.

You can see by looking at me that I lost my arm; it was something terrible I don't want to remember now. That hospital was the most horrible place I'd ever seen in my life. There was so many wounded from the fight that it was nearly noon of the next day before they finally got to me.

The surgeon didn't even tell me what he was going to do. He stuck his finger into the bullet hole and I could feel the splinters of bone in there just rubbing and grating. I tried to hold back from screaming. I remember begging him to make me better so I could get back with my regiment because they needed me. He motioned to a man standing behind me and they placed a towel over my face that smelled really sweet. I woke up an hour later and my left arm was gone just below the shoulder.

That was when I truly wanted to die. To just go to sleep and find myself with Pa and Jim.

I was sick for a long time, I guess. It wasn't just the arm; a bullet had creased my head as well and gave me a bad concussion, like the one I had when I was little. I was wounded in the heart as well. Not by a bullet; it's just I think that too much had happened. Losing Jim, seeing all the men dying, the dead Rebel boy, and losing the battle as well. I guess I was in there a week or more when I woke up and saw Colonel Russell standing in our hospital tent with Sergeant White beside him, talking to some of the wounded. When the colonel saw me looking at him, his eyes just got really bright and he came over to sit on the edge of my bed.

"Hello there, Sam, how you doing?"

I didn't say anything. I just looked up at him.

He smiled sadly.

"You had us all worried there for a while that you just weren't going to wake up."

He sighed.

"I heard about Jim. He was a good soldier; we'll miss him."

I still didn't talk.

He reached out and took my good hand.

"I know, Sam. I know."

I could see the tears in his eyes. They were tears for everything, for all of us, including me. I started to cry again, feeling ashamed to be crying in front of my colonel like that. But he was crying too, and I guess the sight of the two of us got near everyone else in the tent upset as well.

The whole time he kept ahold of my hand until I was just cried out.

"Now how about a cup of coffee. I want to talk with you for a minute," he said softly.

I nodded; he left the tent and came back in a minute later with two cups of steaming coffee. He sat down again, and helped me to sit up a little bit. He didn't feed me the coffee; he insisted that I do it myself, though he did steady my hand a bit.

It tasted wonderful and I think with that cup I felt like wanting to live again.

"When can I get back with the regiment?" I finally asked.

He looked at me and tried to force a smile.

"You're going home, Sam; your war's over."

I tried to take that in and it left me empty.

"The regiment's my home, it's all I got," I whispered.

"Sam, don't you have parents, a home?"

I shook my head.

"Jim was all I got. We ran away together. Pa's dead, Ma got sold south."

He lowered his head.

"Damn this war," he whispered and then he stirred again, looking at me closely and forcing a smile.

"Captain McHenry and Sergeant Felton told me all about you," he finally said. "Told me you were a regular hero, that you fought like a tiger."

"We lost, though, didn't we, Colonel," I whispered. "We lost."

He shook his head.

"Sure, maybe a battle. Maybe someday you'll have people telling you what a horrible, mixed-up affair it was. But you, the men of my regiment, your people, you didn't lose anything, son. By God, you won."

He looked around at the other men in the tent.

"I'm proud of all of you. Honored that I had a chance to lead you and stand by your side. By God, in my book, it was worth it."

He looked back at me.

"It was worth it, Sam, it was worth it."

I guess now that it was. I think we proved something not only to our country but to ourselves as well. You see, for the rest of my life I was never afraid of anything ever again. I knew in my heart I was no longer a slave, that I bought a part of this country with my blood.

The colonel finally left me, saying that he'd make sure I was well taken care of. Later that day they loaded me onto a hospital boat that took me back to Washington. I was sick on and off for a couple of months. The stump of my arm didn't heal right and got all infected twice over. But finally I started to mend.

Early into the fall I was sent back to Indianapolis and there waiting at the train station for me was Miss Latimer. She'd received a letter from the colonel about me and she was all in tears when I got off the train. At least I was able to walk, but I was still kind of shaky.

The following day I was honorably discharged from the army and told I'd have a pension of ten dollars a month for the rest of my life from the State of Indiana.

That winter was mighty hard. Auntie Hubbard took me back into her boardinghouse and refused to take more than a dollar a week. Mr. Speed found me some work that needed writing. I realize now he could have done it a lot easier himself but he wanted to help and knew I wouldn't take charity. Every afternoon and evening I went to school. There was, after all, my promise to Jim.

The war ended the following year. The old 28th was in at the end of it and had the honor of being one of the first regiments to storm into the Rebel capital of Richmond. I got a letter from Sergeant White telling me how proud a moment it was, our troops charging down the street past the Confederate Capitol Building, every black man and woman in Richmond pouring into the streets, shouting that they were free.

He said it was the proudest moment of his life, that he thought of me and all the other men who had been wounded or died. It was a year late in the coming, he said, but the 28th

United States Colored Troops were in at the end, helping to win the war and set our people free.

There isn't much more to tell now. It took a long time to heal on the inside. I had terrible nightmares and still do at times. Usually they're about Jim, or all the comrades of my regiment who died or, worst of all, that Rebel boy dying in front of me. I did cheer up a bit when in January 1866 my regiment came home to Indianapolis to be discharged. They paraded down Market Street and everyone in the city, black and white, all of us free, came out to see them. I managed to put my uniform back on, though I'd grown a bit, and went down to the station to meet them.

Colonel Russell, who was now a general, saw me when he got off the train and, by God, he saluted me. I saluted back and he ordered me to fall in with my regiment for the review and march alongside him, right up at the front of the parade.

So I got to march with my regiment one last time as we paraded up Market Street. Behind me the drums were rolling and again I felt that shiver down my spine. We held a big celebration that night and then one by one the men left and started for their homes, promising we'd see each other again. Some of them I did, like Sergeant Major Felton, Major Garland White, who was one of the first black officers in the history of the United States, and General Russell, but a lot of the men just disappeared back into civilian life, which is, I guess, the way it's supposed to be.

Our torn and bloodstained flags were sent to the statehouse and put behind a glass case, with a stack of muskets and a single drum behind them.

I finally took a full-time job as a clerk in Mr. Speed's business and kept on going to school. A year and a half later I got a letter from General Russell, who was now a lawyer, saying that he was in touch with a General Howard, who was starting a college up for blacks in Washington, D.C. He said both Pastor White and he were recommending me for the school and if admitted, since I was a wounded veteran, I could go for free.

That fall I left Indianapolis. Six years later I came back with a wife, my first son, and a degree to practice law, something I've been doing these last twenty-three years. In my little office hangs a photograph of my regiment. You can just barely see me in it, and there alongside me, as I guess he's been even after all these years, is my cousin Jim.

I fought my first battle for my people in a forgotten little skirmish near the crossroads of White House, Virginia, and lost my arm to the cause at the Battle of the Crater. I'm fighting for them today by using the law.

Yet even after all these years, when it gets still at night, and I sit on the porch, I can almost hear the voices of my long-gone comrades as we marched down the roads of Virginia, singing and laughing. I can still hear that song that we sang: *We looks like men a marchin' on, we looks like men of war.*

I kept my promise to Jim, I kept my promise to my pa and ma, and most of all to my people and my country. Next year I think I'll march in the parade again, and maybe someday I'll march in the front of it, the way the colonel had me do when we came home.

I'll never forget all those men who are no more, who died for a word called *freedom*. It's something everyone has to fight for, I guess, because freedom has to be won new each morning, and guarded each night, and it's a dream that I hope shall never die.

Historical Note

★   ★   ★

The Real Story of the
28th United States Colored Troops

The 28th United States Colored troops was a real regiment, one of over a hundred and eighty black regiments that served with the Northern armies in the last two years of the Civil War.

At the start of the war the idea of black regiments was not a popular one and many questioned whether such troops would fight. This thinking demonstrates yet again the way history is often forgotten, since thousands of soldiers of African descent fought gallantly in the American Revolution and again in the War of 1812.

By late 1862, thinking started to change, if for no other reason than the horrendous casualties being suffered by white troops, and the fact that it was becoming difficult to find new recruits for the Union cause.

Many now believe that the famous 54th Massachusetts was the first black regiment. In fact, several regiments of black troops had already been formed and saw action prior to the organization of the 54th, including units in Louisiana, South Carolina and Kansas.

By early 1863, the federal government had officially started the raising of black regiments, which were called United States Colored Troops (USCTs). Cavalry, artillery and heavy artillery regiments units were formed as well. The 28th was authorized by Governor Morton of Indiana in the fall of 1863, and the first company was organized in December of that year.

Reverend Garland White, the former slave of Senator Robert Toombs of Georgia, who became a general in the Confederate Army, was instrumental in the creation of the 28th and would eventually become the regimental sergeant-major. In late 1864 Reverend White was commissioned as a major, one of the first of eleven black officers in the United States Army.

The men of the 28th received extensive training and stayed in Indiana until April 1864. Their officers were white, almost all of them combat veterans who were well trained and dedicated to their regiment.

The 28th was assigned to service with the Union Army of the Potomac, fighting against Robert E. Lee's Army of Northern Virginia, and the experiences that our characters Sam and Jim went through follow the historical record of that regiment from its creation up to the Battle of the Crater, fought on July 30, 1864.

The Battle of the Crater was a horrible disaster for the Union cause. The men of the 28th were indeed supposed to lead the charge, and were well trained for the attack, but at the last minute the commander of the Army of the Potomac, General George Meade, decided to pull the black units from the attack. To this day there is debate as to his reasoning. Regardless of what motivated him, his decision triggered a debacle. White troops who were not trained for the assault went in first and by the time the black division was committed, the battle was already lost.

The men of the 28th fought with exceptional valor. Examination of their pension records reveals riveting accounts of the valiant but doomed attack. Nearly half the men of the regiment were killed, wounded or captured. A number of men wound up in POW camps and endured ghastly conditions. Seven out of eleven officers were casualties as well.

After the battle the 28th was pulled from the line and kept in reserve, seeing some limited action a couple of months later. At the end of the war, the 28th was directly in front of Richmond, and on the night the Confederate Army evacuated the capital, the men from Indiana claimed the honor of being among the first troops to enter the fallen city.

Major Garland White describes in a letter the excitement he and his comrades felt as they stormed into Richmond, and the wild, ecstatic greeting they received from the liberated slaves of that city. Suddenly, from out of the crowds gathering round the regiment, Garland heard someone crying his name and turned to see his mother pushing forward, flinging herself into his arms. He had not seen her since he had escaped from slavery years before.

The 28th still had a final mission left, and it proved to be one of their toughest. As the Civil War wound down, there was the threat of another war exploding along the Texas border. While America had been immersed in its great crisis, France had invaded Mexico. We were supporting the Mexican army, fighting against the invaders, and fifty thousand Union troops were transferred to the border, over half of them black troops. Their mission was to pressure the French into leaving and prevent the war from spreading into Texas.

For nearly half a year the 28th endured nightmarish conditions: stifling heat, lack of water, the anger of the local population, who saw them as an occupying army, and rations so bad that most of the men came down with scurvy. Dozens of men died from disease and malnutrition.

France finally backed down from its belligerent stance, though their troops would remain in Mexico for three more years. The 28th was at last discharged from federal service, returning back home to Indiana in January 1866.

They returned to a state where these gallant veterans were still denied the right to vote, to own property, to sit on a jury and to send their children to school. But what they had accomplished was a beginning.

Frederick Douglass declared that once a former slave had held a musket, and carried a cartridge box with *U.S.* stamped on its lid, no power on the face of the earth could ever again deny him the rights of citizenship.

The words were prophetic. The heroic service of the men of the USCTs became the first step in the long struggle to full and equal rights in a country that they had so willingly shed their blood for.

After the war, many of the veterans settled in Indiana; a number of them moved to Kansas, where one veteran was still living in the late 1920s; one even wound up working on an English steamship at the beginning of the twentieth century. Their pension records show a remarkable attitude at a time when racism was still rampant. Repeatedly, government officials who interviewed the veterans of the 28th wrote of their heroism, integrity and the moral obligation of our society to do justice to these men who had fought to preserve the Union. Their legacy is a valiant one and should forever be honored by our nation, which they fought to preserve.